DRAGON RISING

The Year of the Ninja Master: Spring

Wade Barker

WARNER BOOKS

A Warner Communications Company

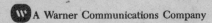

A DARK SHADOW ROSE TO DEFEAT THEM...

BRETT WALLACE

The undisputed Ninja master, whose mission was to destroy lawbreakers and misfits—until forced to fight insanity and his former comrades-in-arms.

JEFF ARCHER

The loyal friend of Brett who must choose between his own life and that of a man hell-bent on destruction.

RHEA TAGASHI

The sensuous, beautiful Ninja mistress from the East whose legendary martial arts skills are matched only by her love for Brett—and her allegiance to the Ninja way.

HAMA

The judge and the warrior ever faithful to the ancient *bushido* code of honor until he is commanded to kill the one man nothing can destroy.

All must oppose each other, while an invisible, insidious evil dares to challenge the Ninjas' might and even control the world in the first deadly season in THE YEAR OF THE NINJA MASTER

DRAGON RISING

TO WARREN MURPHY

"The difference between you and me, kid, is that I know the name of the problems."

Author's Note

All weapons and mythological images are based on actual oriental and South American legend, fables, and history. All ninja lore is based on the research now available.

San Francisco, Mexico, and El Salvador actually exist. Only Wade Barker's name has been changed.

All Japanese and Chinese translations are taken in the Romanized transliteration format.

Arigato, domo, sumimasen.

Hao yunn-chih.

...ening in the funnel. The man's terror prevented
...from hearing the offer of help.
...had almost jumped in after him. But he heard
...counts down the ladder and...

PART ONE

"I hate and I love. Perhaps you ask why I do so. I do not know, but I feel it, and I am in torment."

Catullus, Odes, LXXXV

1

Knives.

Jeff Archer couldn't believe his eyes.

Their silver blades shone in the glare of his flashlight, casting a deadly gleam in the dank cellar. The red crystal LEDs of his digital watch read 4:26 A.M. Brett Wallace was doing two-fingered push-ups in the dark before dawn, over knives.

Brett was not on the floor of the secret basement dojo. He was on a plywood platform atop five cinder blocks, one block at each corner and one supporting the center. He had jammed the knives through the board so that the wide, wicked blades were pointing at the ceiling. He held himself prone over the knives with his arms, and his arms were supported by his rigid fore and middle fingers.

His fingers were on either side of two other blades. These hadn't been jammed through the platform floor. They were held horizontally, two nails hammered on either side of each knife's grip, blade edge up. They were three inches wide, blades that just touched the soft flesh at the base of the two fingers.

Any weakening, and the knives would unavoidably sink into Brett's hands—and into every area of his body. There were blades under his thighs; a blade at his stomach; blades on either side of his chest—positioned so they would slip between his ribs; blades where his pectorals sank toward the floor; and a blade at his throat, a blade that would just touch the skin of his neck each time he slowly lowered himself.

Jeff Archer stood in the doorway of the basement, transfixed, flashlight in hand. He gripped it harder as it began to shake. He quickly looked up the stairs, just to make sure they were alone. The stairway was empty. The Dawn Dojo above them was empty and closed for the night. The San Francisco streets beyond were nearly as quiet.

It was the cusp of the day: a time of rest for those who slept; a time of madness for those awake. Even in all-night towns, the period between four-thirty and six was a time to drift, to ponder, to dream. It was a time to shake off one day and start the next.

But for some—a select few—it was a time to court demons. It was the time of the dead, an eternal pause where your worst fears took on a shadowy life. It was a time to grab for the very fabric of your nightmares, a time when your finger-tips touched something fluttering, fast, and bone-freezingly real.

Most of the time, it escaped. You watched, your heart pounding, as whatever it was streaked deeper into the night, swallowed by the retreating darkness. As the sun rose, you convinced yourself it was imagination. There are no such things as ghosts or devils or demons.

But sometimes, *sometimes* the demon *is* caught. Not by you, never by you. But sometimes the possessed, the *obsessed,* don't pull back. They add the tiniest bit of speed. They don't weaken at the finish. Their fingers claw and grip. And the demon turns and takes form.

Then they know. They know fear and horror have a life force of their own, a presence that can be touched. It never leaves them, then. Reality is no longer predictable or controllable. It is a fight—where the stakes can be more than one's individual life.

Jeff Archer raised the beam of his flashlight. Brett Wallace's face rose and fell in it. He did not look toward the light, but Archer could see that his eyes glowed for a second. He had been blinded. Yet he did not stop, did not stiffen, did not even slow. He maintained the speed of his exercise, lowering and raising himself over the blades.

Archer moved the light away.

"No," said a flat, quiet voice.

Archer moved the light back. Brett Wallace was smiling. That is, his lips were pulled back from his teeth. His head was turned toward the young man in the doorway, his eyes black, bottomless, and dead, with only a slight glistening to show his eye sockets were not empty.

An icicle shivered down Archer's back. He leaned against the wall.

Brett Wallace continued his push-ups for twenty-four more minutes. Only he knew how long he had been doing them before that. Archer kept his flashlight trained on the same spot all that time. In the last three minutes, Brett had gone down once and come up with a red, drooling dot on his chin. He said nothing. His expression did not change. Nor did his pace.

At four fifty-five, he stopped. He threw his legs up until he was doing a handstand over the blades on four fingers. Then he arched his body and catapulted himself to his feet on the basement floor.

"What do you want?" the young man heard the same lifeless voice ask.

Archer saw the man he had known for five years as the Ninja Master wiping his hands on a paper towel, then throwing it to the floor. He instinctively shone his light on it. The crumpled, absorbent paper showed dark stains.

Archer wanted to say many things. He wanted to pour out his concerns. But you didn't say such things to Brett Wallace now. Still, Archer owed too much to him not to speak the truth.

"I was worried about you," he said simply.

"Your worries are your own battle." Wallace picked up a plastic spray bottle and misted his face.

Archer expected little else in way of reply. Over the last two years, Wallace had turned any acts of caring against his would-be protectors. He seemed uninterested in how anyone else felt.

Jeff was prepared for this. He didn't let it confuse or hurt him. At least, not as much as it had before.

"Your eyes," he said instead. "What happened to your eyes?"

Brett laughed—a humorless, scraping rasp. The laugh seemed to say, "What concern is that of yours?"

Jeff controlled his irritation. Perhaps he was reading too much into Brett's actions.

"I was testing eyedrops," Brett said. "They are supposed to help you see in the dark. They only aggravate the nerves."

"Oh," said Jeff, walking over from the door. "That explains it."

"That explains *what?*"

Jeff was taken aback. Brett seemed to be baiting him.

"You were working out in the dark."

"I prefer to exercise in the dark." Wallace stared at the younger man.

"Why?"

"Why?" Wallace echoed as if it were the stupidest

question he had ever heard. *"Because there is no light."*

"But . . ."

"There is no light!" he repeated with vehemence. "You think the sun shines at your convenience? You think the heavens respond to you at the snap of your fingers?"

"Brett . . ." Archer began carefully.

"Don't call me that!" he snapped. "I am *genin*, ninja operative. I serve my lord's wishes."

"You are *nuts!*" Jeff said. He had had it. He wasn't going to tippy-toe around Wallace's lunacy the way Rhea and Hama did. That wasn't why Brett had taken him as a student. That wasn't what Brett had taught him the last five years.

Brett Wallace looked at Archer, his expression flat. "You want light," he said. He walked, unhurried, to a small table while Jeff followed him with the light. Covering it was every manner of *shuriken*, the ninja throwing star: three-pointed, four-pointed, six- and eight-pointed stars; edges straight, curved, and triangular; shining silver, gold, or black metal; some with holes in the middle, some without.

There were only two things they had in common: they were store-bought—every martial arts shop in the city had dozens of them; and they had been sharpened by Brett in his workshop. The edges were as thin and sharp as he could get them, and there was sandpaper-like pebbling along the edges that felt like grit under the fingers.

Brett gathered a handful, ignoring the sharpened

points, and moved around the room throwing them toward the opposite wall.

Jeff heard them traveling in the dark like whips or slow bullets. They sounded as though they were tearing the air, their passing lined with a shrieking edge, the air crying in pain.

Each hit its target with a deep, resonant thud. It wasn't the reinforced wall they were hitting. They were obviously thunking into some sort of target—a thick wooden target. One after another Brett would hurl them toward the wall, wasting no motion but packing an extraordinary amount of strength behind each one. The velocity didn't vary. Each *shuriken*'s power was the same. Each bit into the target and sank.

Jeff could see there was no talking to Brett tonight—no rational conversation, at any rate. He had been worried about Brett. All right: he had found him, and he was fine. But he had started something tonight, something that they would have to finish. For months he had been afraid of Brett. He had been frightened that the Ninja Master had gone insane. But not tonight. Tonight the fear had only strengthened his resolve. He had begun his fight for the Ninja Master.

Jeff Archer looked away and started toward the door.

"Don't move," Brett commanded. Archer stopped and turned his light toward the voice. Wallace's face was covered in sweat. His arm lashed out again and again. Jeff saw frustration in Brett's expression. Brett finally weaved, anchored his footing, and threw his last *shuriken*, using the full length of his arm.

The star spun vertically across the room, dipped, and sank into the target horizontally—with just the smallest of sparks.

Then the spark multiplied upon itself until dozens of tiny sparks combined, exploded, and swirled into a small flame.

In that light, Jeff saw the square wooden target affixed to the wall. On it were tacked open packs of matches. Each *shuriken* had sunk just over the match tips. Only the last one was thrown precisely enough to light one pack.

"There," Brett said through clenched teeth. "Light."

Jeff knew he was angry that he hadn't been able to do it while bobbing. He had had to plant his stance and aim. But that didn't explain *why*.

The oriental man in the white smock screamed.

It was the sound that drilled through Rhea Tagashi's ears every morning at the wharf; like a fistful of nails, their nails scraping across a blackboard—amplified a hundred times.

She hated that sound. The shrieking Chinese language was so disgusting. She looked at Hama beside her—burly, squat, and bald as a honeydew. As always, he was imperturbable. His brow was not furrowed in concentration. Then again, he was only the cook. He could only suggest which fish she should buy. Rhea was the owner. *She* made the final decision.

And Rhea was a beautiful businesswoman as well as shrewd. She stood out in the crowd despite her diminutive five-foot, hundred-pound frame. Her coal black hair was held by a simple ivory comb and cascaded down her back to her wasp waist. She had almond eyes and skin of silk, high, proud breasts, and an air of refinement. She did not relish having to deal with the Chinese and Vietnamese fishermen.

The oriental in the white smock screamed for his young oily-faced assistant to bring forth the *good* salmon for "Missy Tagagoshee" to consider.

Rhea waved him away, anxious to move on after having seen his sorry catch. The Chinese fisherman kept motioning her frantically to stay just one second more. Rhea spun on her sneakered heel and walked away. The assistant scurried after her with a two-foot-long salmon, but Hama stepped in front of him, his own sneakers sliding on the sea-slickened stone of the wharf. He shooed the disappointed boy back to the stand where the fisherman screeched at him, his arms waving.

Everywhere fishermen were shrieking. Their bumblebee voices wore on Rhea's nerves. Theirs was a coarse scraping compared to the guttural poetry of the Japanese language. Everything about the Chinese was insectlike: their words, their manner, their number. They were a hive of bees, all sharing the same mind, all working toward the same end, all buzzing incessantly.

"I don't know how I stand it," she said, moving to the next stall.

"Neither do I," Hama replied noncommittally, not caring to ask what Rhea was talking about.

She couldn't tell whether he was being sarcastic. He seemed absorbed in the search for today's seafood. There had been a number of incidents with bad tuna in the city recently, with huge lawsuits against several sushi bars coming to trial. Hama, seemed—*seemed*, that is—to be concentrating on the effort to prevent the same from happening to the Rhea Dawn Restaurant.

But they both knew what was really bothering her. And they both knew he was busying himself in his work to take his mind off the same thing.

A single English-speaking voice broke the Chinese cacophony.

"Hello, Rhea." Jeff Archer had appeared at her shoulder. "Hama."

Jeff looked like the archetypical all-American boy, clearly out of his element in the crowd of orientals. He stood just under five foot nine, had light brown hair and regular, handsome features. One could believe he was still in college; he had that perpetual youthfulness that persists in some men to middle age, although in Jeff's case he was just the other side of thirty. Today his usual easy smile had been replaced by a look of purposefulness.

"Jeff," Rhea said evenly, showing no surprise. Two years ago she would have hugged and kissed him. Today she didn't even shake his hand.

"Not here, Jeff," Hama said immediately, his attention focused on the young man even while he examined some shrimp. "Not now."

But Archer was not to be put off. *"We have to talk,"* he said with whispered intensity.

Rhea opened her mouth but Hama spoke first. "There is nothing for us to talk about."

Rhea hoped Hama was trying to spare her feelings. Why else was he so intent on ignoring Brett's change in character? He must know how Rhea felt about Brett, beyond the respect and honor members of a ninja family bestow on one another.

But as quickly as her emotions softened, she realized that a ninja could not afford such feelings. There *was* nothing to talk about. What was, was. But Jeff was an American, a Caucasian, a round-eye. They railed against reality. They analyzed, psychoanalyzed. Archer could no more understand ninja than could one of these dead carp that littered the wharf.

Archer grabbed Hama's arm and spun the Japanese man around to face him. Hama allowed it, his face calm, his expression closed.

"I know what is happening here," Jeff said slowly into the bland, lineless face, his eyes locked on Hama's. "I know what you are. We have to talk. Period."

Rhea stepped in. She was between them, both literally and figuratively. She was born ninja. She was Japanese. But, hatefully, she loved Brett Wallace. She loved him with a passion that shamed her heritage. A ninja could know love no more than she could know hate, or any mindless emotion.

"We will talk, Jeff," she promised.

"Today," Archer insisted. He would be delayed no longer. It was getting far too late for that.

"Today," she agreed. "Back at the restaurant."

"Unless you want to chat among the squid," Hama said caustically.

Jeff glared at him. Finally he backed up, looking at Rhea. "As soon as you get back."

She nodded. He stalked off, ignoring the chattering Chinese who swung fish at him as he left. She looked back at Hama, but he was examining the fish in the stall intently.

Rhea Tagashi stood in the sunrise on the wharf, covered by the stench of dead or dying fish, surrounded by shrieking Chinamen. Alone.

A woman cried; a ninja did not. Rhea did not cry. She ran. Hama and a single Chinaman watched her go.

He felt the head in his hands. Its skull was still intact, but the bones at the neck were cracked and loose. They clicked soundlessly against the skin.

His right leg lay straight on the carpeted floor. He no longer felt any pain when he pulled his muscles into that position, a fact that scared him. His left leg was bent so that he was low to the floor. He held his right arm aloft, a crimson pole bearing the disembodied head. The mouth was open, a dried stream of blood dangling from the chin like a red icicle. The eyes were open, but dead and lifeless.

Anthony B. Merritt raised the gun. The huge revolver belched white flame and bucked, the lead missile spun across the room, and the head erupted, all in slow motion. Then the pieces exploded in all directions at super speed.

The bone, the sinew, the muscle, and the brains splashed into Brett's face. He cringed. He couldn't help it. His body rebelled against the horrid devastation.

He held on. He rose to hurl the shuriken into Merritt's arm. Then he lashed the lawyer's paralyzed body to that of a long-dead girl who smelled of feces and decay, dragged them both to the edge of the deck, and rolled them into the sparkling blue water of a marble swimming pool. He watched and waited as the attorney sank, his mouth open. Huge semicircular bubbles twisted out of his mouth and rose to the pool's surface.

The throat widened, filling with water. The eyes rolled up. The skin darkened. It took forever.

Then the face changed. The skin blackened and flaked off, forming a puddle on top of the water. The eyes rolled all the way over, but they were glassy, faceted blank eyes. The flailing arms and legs grew thin, bent, and doubled. Then tripled. The dead, rotting girl was bound to a bug, a giant insect.

The monstrous insect easily slid from the ropes, sank to the bottom of the pool, and walked up the side of the marble. Then the insect skittered toward Brett, leaped unnaturally onto him, and tore at Brett's face with bile-drooling, clacking, razor-sharp mandibles . . .

Brett Wallace dove forward, slamming onto the

teak floor face first, the bed clothes tangling his legs. His arms just prevented him from ripping the flesh from his chin.

He had fallen off his bed. No, he had *thrown* himself from bed and from his nightmare-scarred sleep. He was gulping for air. Huge beads of sweat dotted his face and torso.

When Jeff returned, Brett was gone. The younger man had walked through the restaurant's dining rooms to the stairs. He had gone up to the balcony where Brett usually ate. He went beyond, up to the loft over the restaurant where Brett lived.

The long table to the right was empty. The bathing enclosure, with its sunken tub, enclosed shower, and Jacuzzi was empty. The platform bed and sleeping mats were empty. Only Brett's closet and bookshelves weren't empty.

The shelves were lined with computer and video equipment. Profits from Brett's parents' real estate holdings as well as from the dojo and restaurant enabled him to keep up with the latest technological advances.

The closets were filled with clothes—but not the clothes of a fashionable man-about-town. These were uniforms mostly: a custodian's coveralls, a mailman's jacket, a three-piece business suit, a doctor's gown.

They were the outfits of invisibility. Brett could go anywhere wearing them. He could infiltrate boardrooms as well as alleys. Everything was part of Brett's art, the art of *ninjutsu*.

Brett had studied in the art for a decade. But he hadn't always been Brett Wallace. Under the name of his birth, he had studied martial arts for nearly a decade before that. It was in this era that he had found his wife. He brought her from Japan to his home and impregnated her, only to lose his entire family to drug-maddened murderers. They raped and killed her, then slashed his parents to death and wrote slogans on the walls.

The man who was to become Brett Wallace went insane. He saw the murderers captured, tried, and released on a technicality before killing them himself. He escaped arrest by returning to Japan. There he achieved a strange tranquility by giving himself to a ninja school.

Ten years later he returned to America with a new name, Brett Wallace, and a new purpose. He wanted to seek justice for those as wronged as he. He tried, only to succumb to the decadent and hedonistic American life-style. He tried to be a superhero: "fighting crime" while enjoying his wealth and machismo.

His new parents, his lords and masters, his *sifus* and *senseis*, had to bring him back to Japan where he learned that the ninja was not a club he could join at will and quit at whim. It was a life, his life. It was a family, his family. And it was unforgiving.

His retraining was merciless. If he had failed at any juncture, he would have been dead.

But he did not fail. He was reborn into his ninja life. In deference to that, he was given his soul: the swords, the ninja fighting swords so keen they could cut a man from shoulder to hip without slowing.

Wallace returned to America, and he fought. But as he fought greater and greater evil, he saw that his original intent had become a bottomless pit, a winnerless battle. For every killer he killed, for every rapist he destroyed, for every pusher he punished, there were dozens of others.

Society bred them in ever-increasing numbers. Money and passion drove them to ever more outrageous crimes. He was like lightning: devastating and deadly when striking, but rare. The chances of being hit by lightning were a million to one. The chances of being slashed by the Ninja Master were equally remote. He served a purpose, but it wasn't enough. Worse, it hardly seemed necessary.

There was too much evil in the world. There were too many victimizers. He had fought again and again, but there was never an end. Even worse, he never seemed to make progress. He stayed in place and fought, like a whirring blender, until he couldn't tell who or what was evil anymore.

Brett Wallace went insane a second time. He had looked into the face of evil only to see his reflection.

"Jeffrey?"

Archer looked down the stairs to see Rhea standing on the balcony. "You wanted to talk?"

"Where's Hama?" he asked, coming down.

"Here," the burly Japanese replied. He had been sitting cross-legged at the head of the low, chairless table, out of sight.

Jeff ignored the man. "Is Brett still having nightmares?" he asked Rhea, facing her.

"I wouldn't know."

"Come on, Rhea!" Jeff barked angrily.

"I know as much about his life today as you know about his training," she said defensively. Archer had to admit to himself that he knew almost nothing about the purpose behind Brett's recent exercises.

There was a time they had trained together. No more. Brett trained while Jeff taught martial arts classes and slept.

"You know nothing?" Jeff asked incredulously.

"He has . . . shut me out," she said carefully.

"What does that mean?" Archer retorted irritably.

"He has thrown her out of his life, his work, and his bed," Hama interjected cruelly. She flashed him a hateful look, then redirected her anguish at Jeff.

"I thought you wanted to talk," she said, "not interrogate." She flushed and then turned away.

"Satisfied?" Hama asked lightly.

Jeff turned on him. "All right, then. It is as bad as I thought."

"Nothing is bad. Nothing is good. What is, is," Hama said with veiled eyelids.

"Stow it, Confucius," Archer said angrily. "Let's see if our stories match. Two years ago, almost to the day, Brett Wallace walked out of the Cannon Crossing Gun Club. We were wounded—physically. I think it's safe to say he was wounded mentally."

Hama opened his mouth. Jeff cut him off.

"Whatever the reason, he was not the same Brett Wallace who walked in."

"Those men," Rhea broke in. "I think he saw too many similarities between what those men were doing and what he . . . we were doing."

What "those men" were doing was trying to mete out justice to the "kind of people" who had raped and murdered their own families. The only things that distinguished the Ninja Master from members of The Revenge House were his far superior killing abilities and his certainty of his victims' crimes. The gun-clubbers were shooting and raping anyone they thought might be a pimp, pusher, mugger, or hooker.

"A man does not go crazy," said Hama. "He either is or he isn't."

"I said shut up," Jeff said carefully. "The situation is bad enough—that's right, bad—without you breaking open a fortune cookie every other minute."

"Fortune cookies are Chinese gimmicks," Hama said with disgust.

"Damn it, Hama, shut your fucking mouth!" Archer yelled. "You just sit and wait and watch, don't you? You're just biding your time until the word comes down from on high."

Hama's eyes opened. Then they all but closed again. "Whatever do you mean?" he asked with clipped tones.

"You don't have to play dumb." Archer scowled. "For the past twenty-four months, Brett has separated himself from all of us and hasn't stopped working. He either is doing research upstairs or is in training. He only stops to eat, sleep, or shit."

"And he does precious little of that," Rhea said quietly. She had sat at the table, as far away from Hama as she could without facing him from the other end.

"All right," said Jeff, straightening. "Brett called himself *genin* tonight."

Hama raised his eyebrows. "That's right," Jeff continued. "*Genin*. Operative. He had thought of himself as *jonin* previously; leader, planner, strategist. He obviously thinks that someone else is in control."

Archer paused, waiting for any reaction from the others. None was forthcoming. "I owe Brett a lot," Jeff finally went on. "But I knew what I was getting into. I knew all about the ninja."

Hama chortled. "You've been reading the books and magazines, Jeff? You've been seeing the movies and watching the television shows?"

Jeff ignored the derision in Hama's question. He got to his knees next to Rhea and across from Hama. "Brett is right. Someone . . . *something else* is in control. The ninjas are not schools. They are families, like the American Mafia."

"Oh?"

"You know what I mean, Hama. They've been that way since five hundred A.D., when they flourished during the samurai period."

"Were you there then, Jeff?"

"Neither were you, Hama."

"At least I grew up on the same continent."

"I'm not professing to be one. I'm just telling

you what I know and trying to explain what might be happening to Brett."

"Very good," Hama said. "Go on." With those four words, Hama took control of the conversation. He was now a shogun listening to a report from a peon.

Archer refused to let it frustrate or silence him. "The ninja families flourished in the samurai era to do jobs the samurai could not do because of their code of honor. They were necessary: the samurai were as corrupt and lustful as anyone, only they kept themselves in tighter control. But to allow the ninja to exist, the samurai, the warlords, the shogun, and even the emperor had to think of them as less than human, as mere hired assassins without honor or standing in the rigid society. In that era, honor was everything. The ninja had none."

Archer paused. "So?" Hama inquired. Jeff had taken back the conversation.

"So," he said, "Brett Wallace has realized this. He has realized that the ninja philosophy was created to fill empty, directionless lives. It is a code of honor created in retrospect to give lives of endless murder meaning."

Hama applauded twice, sharply. Jeff Archer turned to the bowed head of Rhea Tagashi.

"Brett Wallace is trying to make himself less than human. He is the head of a ninja family that does not exist. He is the servant of a warlord that is only in his imagination. He is fighting for no one and for nothing. But he cannot stop fighting."

Jeff Archer stood at the end of the table. He looked down at the bald Japanese man. Hama's expression was, as always, noncommittal.

"And if he does not stop," Jeff announced. *"You are going to kill him."*

2

Brett Wallace pumped gas. He cleaned windshields. He checked the oil and tire pressure. He wore a blue shirt with a red, white, and blue Mobil patch over the right pocket, and he wore it with seeming pride.

He had gotten it from a work-clothes catalog in preparation for that very day. He told the two other attendants at the station that he was replacing Mitch for his shift. Mitch was at home, sick. That was true as far as it went. It was all a matter of perspective. Mitch was at home and he was in bed. But Brett had made him sick by putting something in his coffee and his juice, and in every one of his glasses and cups. Brett was not taking any chances.

The weed of crime bore bitter fruit, the Ninja

Master knew. He had become used to the long periods of surveillance and reconnaissance that went with his responsibilities. He had come to relish this research as the most meaningful part of his life. Locating the problem took skill. Cutting it out was simply a hack job any butcher could do.

Well, almost any. When Mitch came down with whatever Brett gave him, Brett put him to bed and washed out every glass and cup. He threw away the bad coffee and bad juice. He kept the remainder of the beige powder he had mixed in the dojo lab in his pants pocket.

The lab and the workshop had grown over the last seven years. By now it was very sophisticated and Brett was very good with drugs and poisons. Before he left Mitch's apartment, he looked into the bedroom. Mitch was snoring fitfully, his face flushed. He would awaken tired—with a headache, but otherwise none the worse for wear.

All right, maybe he would get cancer in thirty years. No one could tell anymore.

The two others at the gas station didn't question the situation. The big boss wouldn't come on until four that afternoon, and if Mitch wanted to lose money to a replacement, that was fine by them.

In fact, they liked this new guy a lot. He was a much harder worker than Mitch. He took on almost all the customers. And since they weren't working for tips, it was no skin off their noses if the guy wanted to give everyone personal service. It gave them all the more time to loaf and watch the passing parade. They were in luck. Today the parade had a float and a marching band. The band was the usual horde of press people. The float was made up of *reputed* crime boss Carlo Ambodini, his lawyer, and his bodyguards.

They all came pouring out of the police station across the street like bees out of a fallen hive. The newsmen did all the buzzing—barking at Ambodini, at the lawyer, at the accompanying cops, at their film crews, and at each other. Ambodini wasn't going to give a press conference later, as all polite mass-murderers do, so they were forced to film and present various "no comments."

Ambodini, the reputed crime lord, had allegedly gone straight. *Reputed* and *alleged* were words introduced by the media in response to the courts' concern for defendants' rights. Things did not exist anymore, they were reputed or alleged to exist. Ambodini was now more involved with mainstream business affairs than numbers and rackets. At the top of his crown was the international heroin trade. Lining the foundation were corporation loans.

The gas station attendant with the gray eyes and sandy hair took a credit card from a patron. He slipped into the gas station office to carefully hone the credit card edge with the knife he kept in his ankle scabbard.

The other attendants walked to the edge of the street to witness the cattle drive. Brett was supposed to be presenting the credit card slip to the customer for signature, but he sauntered over to join them. Ambodini's limousines were at the curb. His men scurried forward to open the door for him. They parted to let him in. He stood straight and turned his head to wave at the reporters.

Brett removed the credit card from the plastic holder and flipped it backhand across the street.

The other gas jerks remembered the angry whistling of the plastic card as it sliced through the air, the white blur with a red streak bisecting it. It disappeared in midair milliseconds after it left Brett's fingers. They turned as he stepped back and ran. Then they returned their gazes to Ambodini.

He had a plastic card stuck in his neck.

It was embedded in the left side, right in the carotid artery. Ambodini kept smiling. He hadn't heard the angry buzzing. He just felt the bee sting. When he slapped his neck, the spray of blood that erupted from above his collar reached over the limo's roof.

Suddenly Ambodini wasn't there. He had sunk from sight behind the car, and the reporters crowded in to get historic videotape of his death. In newsrooms all over the country, reporters would remain professionally dispassionate at the scene of Ambodini kicking his legs and choking himself. But they would be all too aware of the great ratings the "film at eleven" would bring.

"Hey!" two attendants heard behind them. "Hey!" They turned to see a red-faced patron scrambling out of his car. "That fucker just ripped off my antenna!"

The attendants stared at where the man was pointing. Mitch's replacement was in the office, with something shiny in his hand. He chopped down twice at the antenna he had laid on the office desk, then came outside and scooped up the air hose. A long metal tube had been attached to the tire chuck, a tube fashioned nights before to fit precisely. Mitch's replacement slid the antenna down the tube and ran into the street, dragging the hose behind him.

It stretched until he was midway across the right-hand lane. The group on the other side of the limo were running around like scared rabbits. Only Ambodini's lawyer, always alert, was screaming at the bodyguards and pointing toward Brett.

The air hose was controlled by a grip-trigger. Brett had turned the air pressure all the way up after killing Ambodini. Now he squeezed the trigger. The makeshift weapon acted like a cross between a spear and a blowgun. The antenna sped across the street.

He was aiming for the lawyer's neck or ear, but the antenna slammed into the attorney's skull just above the ear. The lawyer's head jerked. He danced sideways, then crumpled next to his client who was still spray-painting the limo's interior with every beat of his fading heart.

A reporter tripped over her own microphone wire while throwing up. The bodyguards scurried back to avoid the noxious gunk. Brett laughed. It was too funny, too outlandish to be taken seriously. Let them try to report this with a straight face on "Eyewitness News." He ripped the pipe off the air hose and ran down the street.

He ran straight for an oncoming bus.

The reporters and the gas station attendants pointed at him. Only the bodyguards went after him. The cops were too busy controlling the crowd. Brett continued to smile as he raced toward the bus with all his speed. The bus driver looked at the man in shock. He twisted his head. There was a car beside him. He couldn't swerve that way. He looked beyond Brett. There was another car coming the other way. He couldn't swerve that way either, unless he wanted a head-on collision.

The bus driver was good. He considered the situation and took the only logical way out—he hit the brakes. Brett dove as the bus screeched to a halt, crawled under it, and slid forward until he reached the manhole cover. He stuck his fingers into the cover's holes and pulled up with all his strength. The heavy iron lid rose far enough for him to get the pipe under it. Wallace pried it off completely and scrambled down the ladder. He landed on a narrow walkway. In either direction stretched miles of tunnels.

It was the Frisco underground. Brett tore off his shirt.

On the street the bodyguards surrounded the bus, waving their .357 Magnums. The bus passengers cringed at the sight of the blue- and silver-plated revolvers with their dark rubber and gleaming brown grips. The bus driver was too petrified to respond to their many directions for a few seconds, then he carefully edged the bus forward.

The men ducked under the bus bottom even as

it moved, trying to locate the insane assassin in the red-dotted sights along their five-inch barrels. They saw the open manhole when the vehicle finally crawled out of the way. The police couldn't stop two men from climbing down. They stopped the rest of the bodyguards and barked into their walkie-talkies.

The two men descended into another world. Brett had scouted the spot well. Only that manhole connected to the sewer system. The others were water tunnels or telephone connections. The stench was incredible. A thick channel of watery bile drifted by them as they stood on the four-foot-wide cement walkway. At their feet was a Mobil shirt, a pair of blue polyester pants, and a pair of cracked brown loafers.

"He must've gone this way," whispered one of the bodyguards.

"He could've gone this way too," said the other, motioning around the corner just next to him.

They both looked down the walkways, the tunnel illuminated by pale, naked yellow light bulbs strung high on the wall.

"All right, let's split up," said the first. "Shoot on sight."

"You bet your ass I'll shoot on sight," said the other, cocking his gun. He walked around the corner. The first man peered into the dimness ahead, crouching. He walked tentatively forward. Brett erupted from the sewage, grabbing the man's ankles. He placed his *tabi*-covered feet on the walkway's side and pulled.

The man's feet were swept out from under him.
He fell heavily on his back, his gun going off. Brett
hardly heard it. He dove forward, knocking the
man's gun hand aside with his knee. He rammed
the metal tube under the bodyguard's sternum
and into his heart.

The man had shouted. Now he exhaled. A tiny,
gravel-tinged groan punctuated his last sound. Brett
grinned, his face covered in dark muck. He could
feel the life leaving the man. Out of the pipe came
an eruption of blood, as from a water main just
turned on. Brett ducked to the side, out of the
way. The blood spurted once more, then dribbled
from the pipe end onto the man's pants.

The other bodyguard ran from around the corner.
Brett somersaulted off the dead man, neatly grabbing the corpse's gun as he landed in a crouch next
to the body.

The second bodyguard did not see Brett. He
just saw something dark moving over his buddy's
prone body. He fired wildly at it. Brett knelt,
pointed the gun barrel as if it were his finger, and
pulled the trigger of the revolver.

The metal "finger" was pointed at the guard's
chest. The bullet slammed through the man's jacket,
and at that range, through his bulletproof vest.
The bullet slowed enough to save him from death,
however, at least temporarily. He dove backward
and fell heavily, sliding on the cement.

Brett could tell from the way the man was
moving that the bullet had not killed him. He
knew he couldn't get a killing angle with the guard

in that position, so he threw the gun into the sewage and pulled up the tight black leggings he wore. Then he pulled the black dagger from its sheath around his calf. It was what he used to sharpen the credit card and sever the antenna, making one a *shuriken* and the other a silver spear.

Brett raced forward as the second bodyguard struggled to a sitting position. One hand held his bleeding chest, the other pointed the shaking gun. Brett threw the knife sideways. It hit the man in the face and bounced off, but not before opening a cut across his eye and nose. The man screamed.

Brett ducked beneath the aim of the gun barrel and got close enough to kick the gun from the panicked man's hand. He swung his forearm across the bodyguard's slashed face. The crying, screaming man rolled sideways and fell into the sewer. He floundered, waving his arms and bawling.

Wallace's smile disappeared. It was the moment in the incredibly violent, mindless cartoon where the main character grabbed at his head and screamed *"What am I doing?!"*

Brett fell to his knees.

"Take my hand," he shouted, holding his arm out to the terrified bodyguard. The man was oblivious, the slowly moving garbage dragging him away. "Take my hand!" Brett bellowed, his voice echoing in the tunnel. The man's terror prevented him from hearing the offer of help.

Brett almost jumped in after him. But he heard the sounds of others coming down the ladder and knew it would be the cops this time. He couldn't rationalize killing cops, no matter how far gone he was. Brett looked over his shoulder. He could see the cops' shadows on the walkway. He looked back. The bodyguard was gone. All he saw beyond his arm was the sewage bathed in repellent yellow light.

His arm was trembling. He fell back against the wall. He felt a layer of perspiration on his face.

His name was Kenneth Christian. He was a madman who had personally killed a score of victims and ordered the loathsome murders of many others for no reason other than to kill. Brett felt his sword—his soul—in his hand, his cleansing, sharp soul. He had driven the blade between Christian's legs. He had felt Christian's bones and organs breaking and tearing under his soul's strength. He knew each sinew of Christian's body intimately. He knew the feel of the blade passing through his intestines, his ribs, his heart, his larynx and tongue, his skull and brain. He had pushed, then pulled, and swung the blade—his soul—free. Christian had been torn in two, his soul a white mist curling up from his gut-flecked hair.

The body flopped into halves. The guts fell, but they were not guts. They were thousands of bugs, spilling out of and over Christian. They skittered so fast Brett could hardly see them. They were a stain, a shadow on the floor, coming right at the Ninja Master. He brought up his soul to smite them, but they went under his clothes and up his

*legs. Those that did not burrow into his sphincter
crawled through his mouth, his nose, his ears.
They crawled inside him and tore him apart.*

Brett Wallace looked to his left. A blue-uniformed
leg appeared in the tunnel. Brett fell forward into
the sewage, letting it carry him away. When he
was safely around the bend, he grabbed onto the
side of the walkway and half dragged, half walked
himself to the river.

The bodyguard waited for him. He lay face up
on the grating as the sewage coursed around him.
His eyes were open. One had been ruined by
Brett's knife. The other stared blindly ahead.

Brett knew what had happened. He had died of
shock and blood loss and poisoning. He had died
in horrible pain, slowly. Brett thought the man
probably had deserved that death. He probably
had killed on Ambodini's order many times. He
probably had destroyed many others' lives. It made
no difference. He had died in horrible pain, slowly.
He had died in tears, screaming and praying.

Brett crawled onto the walkway on all fours. He
was sick. He couldn't stop shaking.

He had thrown his soul away. Not just today. He
had thrown his soul away when he walked into
The Revenge House. He had said as much to
Anthony Merritt. "I have given up my soul to kill
you," he had said. He had tortured and killed
Merritt, hoping to kill a part of himself. It had not
worked.

It was said that when a samurai's soul turned,

so did his sword. But Brett Wallace was not samurai. He was garbage, and he used garbage to escape and kill. Brett crawled out of the sewer and fell into the river. He washed the stench from himself in the polluted water of the river. He soaked his black long-sleeved T-shirt and black pants in the river. He tried to wash his sins away in the river.

He let the river current drag him away from the police . . . and the dead.

"You *have* to kill him."

Jeff Archer remained rooted to the spot. He stared directly into Hama's slitted eyes. Rhea looked slowly over at the bald man.

"It has started," she said. "None of us knows what he is doing."

Hama agreed lightly. "He is too good at what he does to allow us to follow him."

"I've tried," said Archer.

"So have I," Hama admitted.

"Who knows *what* he's been doing," Jeff said in frustration, kneeling. The confrontation had finally degenerated to a mere conversation. "Who knows who he's been killing? I tell you, I read the papers every day. I watch the news. And in every report I see his hand."

"It is not that simple anymore," Hama ruminated, looking toward the delicate white and rose bud vase sitting on a tiny opening between the balcony eating area and the ceiling of the adjoining kitchen. It was a vertically rectangular opening that Rhea had filled with the lovely hand-painted vase. Every day she had replaced the single bloom. Today, the pink summer petals were wilted.

"For months he did nothing. He went nowhere except to the dojo to train. He stayed upstairs reading and researching. He made stacks of newspaper and magazine clippings. He made binders full of notes. Then he burned them all." Hama kept looking at the dead flower as he spoke.

"He would sleep, only to wake from nightmares," Rhea revealed. "Four months ago he . . . asked me to leave. He asked me to find an apartment of my own."

"His eating habits became irregular," Hama continued. "He would eat bags of uncooked rice, then fast for days. Weeks."

"I decided he was seeing how far he could push his mind and body," Rhea said.

"He's taking greater chances in his training," Jeff told them. "He became more abusive and violent in our sparring. He thought I was holding back. He demanded I try to kill him. I couldn't do it. I . . . I don't know . . . I was sure that if I tried, he couldn't keep himself from killing me." Archer shrugged. "Hurting me real bad, at any rate."

"Inflicting permanent damage," Hama enunciated.

The trio sat, quiet and still. There was nothing more to say then. Everyone knew where the other stood. They pondered the predicament and considered their options.

Finally Jeff spoke. He had asked for the meeting, after all. "Have you been in touch with his *ninjutsu* school?" He almost couldn't say it.

Their silence was Archer's answer.

"What have they instructed?"

Again, silence.

"I have a right to know!" Jeff exploded with honest anger.

Hama closed his eyes and nodded slowly. He resembled Buddha then: calm, diffident, imperturbable.

"Master Torii has made it clear..." Rhea said softly. She couldn't go on.

Jeff had to force the issue. He had to know.

"What? What!"

Hama spoke in Torii's voice, his eyes still closed, his back straight. "'The soul. The soul that is dark but still light. The darkness of death and the light of hope. You are not entering a class, you are embarking on a life where there is no turning back...' The *sensei* made this clear to Brett-san seven years ago."

Archer already knew the answer. "He threw his swords away when he left the gun club. His soul."

"We will not be killing anyone," Hama intoned. "Brett Wallace is already dead."

The dead man's hands broke the surface of the dark green water. He dragged himself out of the oily, clinging river and crawled across the brown grass to the asphalt of an unused road. He rested his cheek on tiny shards of aqua glass. The late afternoon sun dried his long-sleeve black T-shirt, his black pants, and the black *tabi* split-toe slippers.

The dead man dreamed.

Brett Wallace's eyes snapped open. He spun onto his back. The second bodyguard's corpse stood above him. His face was blackened, burned almost beyond recognition. His charred suit dripped excrement and sludge. Brett Wallace saw the slash, the deep white slash across the bodyguard's face. Brett scrambled back, the broken glass and pebbles on the road digging into the flesh of his palms. He looked around. On three sides was the river. On the fourth side was an army of the dead. Brett did not look at them, but he recognized every one: street gangs, homicidal maniacs, corrupt policemen, terrorists.

They were all the people Brett had killed. He had slashed their brains or punctured their hearts or snapped their bones. He had watched them die or felt them die under his fingers. Now they were all coming for him.

They did not shamble. They walked, calmly and purposefully. Their mouths were not drooling bile. Their eyes were not wide and popping out. Their arms were not outstretched. They walked naturally, inexorably, toward him.

Brett Wallace stood. He stretched out his arms and went forward to meet them happily.

The dead man pushed himself off the hot black surface. He stood unsteadily and began his walk into the city, avoiding busy sidewalks. He went down back streets and alleyways, climbed over construction fences, and walked across empty, refuse-strewn lots. He vaulted into tenement windows and moved through slums.

He had it all mapped out in his mind. Ambodini had been the last one. There was no way he could keep this murder a secret. Rhea, Hama, and Jeff would clearly see this one as a signal:

Stop me if you can. The deaths will continue and become more and more and more outlandish until you stop me. I am a soulless man, a zombie, a walking dead, no better than those I kill. But I cannot stop.

Brett could no longer be the executioner for a society that bred people like Ambodini the same way farmers bred livestock, champion steers, or stud horses. What purpose did his executions serve? No dead victim was brought back. No ruined life was mended. The satisfaction of punishment paled with oppressive reality. But he could not stop.

And Ambodini and Ambodini's guards were merely replaced. Future victims were not saved. Other criminals, other killers, other rapists took on their work. Brett was destined to kill their replacements and *their* replacements until . . .

Brett stopped and smiled. He saw a fleeting image in his brain: a ninja madly swinging his red-stained *katana* blade through empty air. Everyone around him was already dead; he had killed the entire world. No more victims. No more victimizers.

Inside the tenement there was a tiny crying. A small, frightened voice sobbed in fear.

Brett Wallace had to stiffen, his mouth open, his hands over his face, until he realized it was not he.

Brett turned his head. The tiny weeping was

clearer now. He followed it up a decrepit, creaking, uneven flight of stairs to a sun-drenched room in the far corner of the deserted tenement's second floor.

Brett could make out words now in the jumbled, distant crying: *candy, Mommy,* and *no*.

Brett looked into the room. The floor was covered in broken plaster. A worn rug, thin as a wafer, peeked out from under its chalk. A rusted bed with a torn mattress was in the corner. On it was a small girl in a pink dress and a man with his pants off.

Wallace staggered back into the hall and stood with his hands pressed against his face. It was another nightmare, he was certain. But he heard the words clearly now.

"I don't want to," said the little girl. "You promised me candy," she said tearfully.

"And you'll get your candy," said the man. "Lots of it. I promise. But you have to do what I say first."

"I want to go home," the girl wailed. "I want my mommy."

The words tore out of her throat. This was not bullshit crying, as so many children do when they want their own way. This was genuine fear.

The man was not swayed. "You can't go home. Your mommy hates you. You have to do this."

Brett Wallace's hands went to his sides. He knelt in the slum hallway, reaching for his knife. It was not there. It was in the sewer with the second bodyguard, and the bugs.

He didn't know if this was nightmare or reality. It made no difference to Brett. He couldn't stop killing, and now he knew why. If he stopped, there would only be the victims and the victimizers. There would be no avenger.

"I don't want to!" the child wailed. "I want to go home!"

"Your house burned down. Your mommy and daddy are dead."

The child's voice was pitiful. "Mommy...? You said, you said she hated me..." The girl was crying so hard she could hardly talk.

"They're dead, little girl. I'm sorry, but they're dead. I'll take care of you now. Just...just do as I say."

Brett Wallace walked into the room. Light was streaming into the enclosure from two windows without glass. Outside, the city was sunny. Inside, the tenement room was infused with light. The man looked at Brett's approach in total amazement. He suddenly grabbed the girl around the throat with his forearm.

"Don't come near me. I'll kill her. I swear I'll kill her!"

Brett took two more quick steps, grabbed the man's wrist, and pulled his arm from the little girl's neck. He lifted the girl by grabbing a fistful of her dress, and put her behind him. In her surprise, she stopped crying. The man pulled his wrist from Brett's grip and cringed against the wall, his arms crossed in front of his face.

"Don't hurt me," he babbled. "I'm sorry. God,

I'm so sorry. I can't help myself. Please help me. Oh God, help me, please."

The little girl's brain struggled to explain the scene for a second. Then she laughed. She pointed at the cringing man and laughed and laughed and laughed.

"He's funny, isn't he?" she said. She knew now. It was all a joke. The man in the three-piece gray suit sans pants was a nice man who wanted to fool her. No one in real life kidnapped little girls and raped them or sodomized them or strangled them or buried them by the side of the road or in their cellars or under their porches. No one was that sick, was he?

The little girl laughed in delight. Brett stood beside her, smiling. The man was funny, wasn't he?

"Go outside," Brett told the little girl. "Wait for me." She nodded and ran out of the room. Brett heard her going down the stairs. He turned back to the child molester on the bed.

"How many children have you done this to?" he asked curiously, with mild interest.

The question caught the man unaware. He actually thought about it. "I don't know," he suddenly bleated. "Too many. I'm sick. I can't help myself."

"Get up," Brett said irritably. "Stop whining."

The man sniffed, lowering his arms. Otherwise he did not move.

"You won't hurt me?"

Brett shook his head.

"You promise?"

Brett nodded.

"You'll get me help?"

Brett looked at him with impatience.

The man slowly moved forward. Brett made room for him. The molester slid off the bed and crouched on his knees in front of the man with the light brown hair, the gray eyes, the black outfit, the medium build.

The child molester blinked. "I'm sorry," he said hopefully, looking up. "I need help."

He was within Wallace's reach now.

"I don't care," Brett said.

And he drove the heel of his palm through the man's nose, killing him instantly

3

When he walked onto the street, the little girl was gone.

The horizon cut the sun in half. It bled red light which filled the street. The light only would last for ten minutes, followed by deepening darkness.

Brett Wallace leaned against the tenement stoop, looking at the pavement. People passed him by. Those who noticed him gave him a wide berth. There were stains on his shirtfront and pant legs.

People learned not to ask questions in big cities, questions like "Are you all right?" or "Is anything wrong?" In Smallville, USA, if a man leaned against a wall, head down, with stained clothes, people might try to help. At least they would not be categorically averse to offering help, would not be in complete fear of their own well-being.

In San Francisco, however, as in Chicago, Detroit, Los Angeles, Miami, Houston, Dallas, New York, and Bigtown, USA, innocent bystanders were all too aware of the dangerous possibilities. If the Good Samaritan wasn't knifed or mugged or raped, and he had the good fortune of getting the person in peril to a police station or hospital, the urban system would require reports in triplicate until everyone choked on red tape or was ground into the system.

Brett Wallace stared at the sidewalk and his own feet. The little girl was gone. He wondered whether she had ever existed. He wondered, if he went upstairs, whether the man would still be there. He wondered if the little girl had wandered the streets, to be hit by a bus or abducted by a carload of joyriders or enticed into a van of child pornographers.

Unlikely; the odds were against it. In a city of three million, only one percent could be classified as criminal. That meant there were only three thousand murderers, rapists, thieves, child molesters, and kidnappers for the little girl to worry about.

Brett chuckled silently. Three thousand. Three thousand to kill in just this one city alone. That made his army of the blackened dead seem small.

Brett looked up, grimacing, into the purple twilight. The streetlights had flickered on. This evening he felt better than he had for months. The killing of the child molester had given him no pleasure. At least, the actual killing hadn't. That he had been there to kill did give him pleasure.

It gave him relief, satisfaction, comfort, a weird sense of restfulness, and a strange sense of cheer. The odds of him—a professional avenger, an experienced assassin—coming upon a single child molester *in the act* of forcing a five-year-old to have sex must have been at least . . . three million to one. It was ludicrous to even think about.

But then, it had happened. It had happened almost immediately after he had murdered a crime lord. It was too ridiculous. Brett no longer had to go looking for it, he was a magnet for it. He no longer needed proof of murder to kill someone. He had murdered many because they were associated with his main targets. They had been willing to consort with evil, so Brett had killed them.

There it was again: that image of a figure in black murdering everyone in the world. It was just a matter of time. A man jaywalks; Brett slices him off at the ankles. A man litters; Brett rams his sword in one ear and out the other. A clerk is abusive; Brett cuts out her tongue. A woman smokes in a public place; Brett slices off her lips.

He was certain it was all ordained. He did not come upon the little girl by accident. Something had led him here. Something greater and stronger was controlling his actions. He would no longer fight it, he would let it take over. Therein, he prayed, lay peace.

He knew what he had to do. In the gathering darkness, Brett headed back to the Dawn Dojo.

* * *

The three of them came out of their doors all at once, nearly colliding like the Three Stooges.

Jeff had seen it on television. It was the first story on the eleven o'clock news. Hama had heard it on the radio in the kitchen. Again it was the first story on the eleven o'clock news. Rhea had read it in her office. After a tough evening on the floor, she was just catching up with the day's newspapers. It was the screaming headline on the first page of the *Examiner*.

Jeff gripped her by the elbow. They stared at each other in wonder, standing among the empty tables of the restaurant. Hama muscled by and ran upstairs, taking the steps three at a time. Jeff was distracted by his action: the burly man moved so gracefully and powerfully. Then he looked back at Rhea's widened eyes.

"It was him," she said in bewildered astonishment.

"No shit, Sherlock," Archer said tightly. "What the hell is he trying to prove? What the fuck does he think he's doing?"

"He's challenging us!" Hama had made his declaration from the stairs. He stood on the steps, dressed entirely in black. He had put on black *tabi* footwear and a black tunic over his T-shirt. On his hands were gloves without fingers: ninja gauntlets that left the palms uncovered and were held on by a cloth ring on the middle finger. In one hand he gripped a black hood. In the other was his *ninja-to*—the ninja straight-bladed sword in its black *saya*, or scabbard.

Rhea and Jeff stared at him for a split second. Then Archer burst out laughing.

"You look like the Pillsbury Doughboy after broiling!" he hooted.

"Yasuru!" Hama used the Japanese word for "archer." He continued spitting out his words in Japanese. "This is not funny! Your *jonin* has lost his mind. He has executed a man in public, in full view of a dozen witnesses!"

"What are you going to do?" Archer replied, also in Japanese. "Hail a taxi in that getup? What are you going to say? 'Take me to the Dawn Dojo. I have to execute my jonin'?"

Hama leaped from the stairs. He landed on the table next to Jeff, executing *iai*, the sword fast-draw. He sliced where Archer's head had been. Jeff somersaulted sideways over the adjoining table, grabbing his own belt. He hadn't reached his feet again when he threw the *shuriken*.

Hama's left hand came up. He caught the *shuriken* on the sword's scabbard.

The two men faced each other. Jeff was still in a crouch, another *shuriken* from his belt holder in his hand. Hama stood on the table, knees bent, scabbard held vertically before him, the sword back.

No one spoke, as much as Rhea wanted to. She wanted to shout "Stop it!" or "We mustn't fight one another!" But she knew neither would work. Jeff might laugh again, and this time without mirth. This ninja family had hit rock bottom. Their leader, their father, their *jonin* had gone insane.

"He has turned his back on us," Hama said, still in Japanese. "He has not only rejected Bushido, the code of honor, he has thrown away his swords. Our duty is clear!"

Jeff smirked—half grimace, half frown. He turned away indifferently. "Get off the table. You look ridiculous."

His own *shuriken* sank into the table next to him. Jeff spun around. Hama was on the floor. The *saya* no longer held the throwing star.

"Now he is not only rejecting us—his clan, his *ryu*—he is threatening the ninja!"

"Our duty is to our *jonin*," said Archer evenly.

"He has rejected us!"

"I will not reject *him*!"

"Archer," Rhea said softly, also in the oriental language. "This murder, this execution of the Ambodini man, has made Brett's intentions clear. He will reveal the true nature of modern ninja if we do not stop him."

Jeff kept his back to them. He would not let them see his face, the face he was attempting to keep expressionless.

"You have seen it, Archer," Hama said quietly, the words like piercing blades in the room. "They make stupid television shows, ludicrous movies, exploitive books. We are a joke to them. A curiosity at best. That is as it should be. No one will believe we truly exist. But if Wallace continues, he threatens to destroy our most valued necessity. Secrecy."

Archer said nothing.

Hama sharply turned to Rhea. "I will not talk to him! I do not have to convince *him*! Our duty is clear!"

Jeff dove backward, running. He planted his hands on a table's opposite edges and threw his body through the air. He landed directly behind Hama as the man stalked toward the kitchen. Hama whirled around, slashing his sword horizontally. Archer had already vaulted over him. The younger man landed in front of the spinning Hama and cartwheeled. He slammed against the kitchen door.

He spun around. Hama's *sho kissaki*—his blade's short point—was against Archer's throat.

"You will not kill him," Archer said softly. "We will confront him."

"It is too late for talk!" Hama raged. "He knew... he knew from the moment his *sensei* brought him back to Japan eighty-five months ago! He would either live as a ninja or die!"

"Are you *ronin?* Have you rejected your own *Bushido?*" Archer barked. Hama gasped, jerking back in surprise.

"You cannot kill a warrior! A warrior must commit seppuku! We *will* confront him. If he refuses to return to the honorable ways of the ninja *ryu* then..."

"Then what?" Hama grinned, lowering his sword. He chuckled, and neatly spun the blade back into its scabbard. "Then what?" he repeated. "We hire a ninja?"

*   *   *

The sparks flew at Brett's eyes. They ricocheted off the plastic goggles and died trying to get to his hands, his muscular, rough-skinned hands that worked with the fire of the welding torch without gloves.

He toiled in the workshop with metal and wood. The fire was reflected in the plastic of his goggles and in his eyes. The smell of garbage and excrement still clung to him. It was as it should be.

The samurai had their Bushido, their code of honor. Through the holes in the Bushido fell the ninja. They were guilty of the subterfuges and excesses the samurai wouldn't dream of. The samurai had their righteousness and their blades. The ninja had their tricks, their poisons, their lies, their traps.

Once, men and women were born ninjas when they were born into the ninja families. Needed by the samurai, but hated because they were needed, they were considered even less than the peasants—the peasants a samurai could kill in the street like dogs. The ninja were insects.

The ninja became hateful even to themselves. Soon they worked not for money, but for promised prestige. They assassinated for a payment of position. Even when they forced their "clients" to make good on their assurances of social stature, they were always marked, marked as ninja. Lower than the low.

A spider or centipede is powerful: it can kill. But it is still an insect.

When the samurai class was destroyed—when

the shogun was usurped and the emperor became
no more than a figurehead—then the ninja's cruelty became common. There was no Bushido to
control anyone. And the ninja were hated all the
more.

Those that had taken on guises as impoverished
farmers or peasants or beggars were the lucky
ones. The once-powerful ninja families no longer
even had their pride to keep them alive, to maintain their hope. They had no place on earth and
they had no place in heaven.

So came the philosophy, the dawn. The medita-
tion, the inner strengths, the hand movements,
the histories, the legends: all were ways to make
the ancient assassins "noble." No more dirty tricks;
being a ninja was an "art."

Brett laughed soundlessly again. Today everything was art. Graffiti is art. Wrapping islands in
paper is art. Taking pictures of being shot in the
arm is art. Anything anyone will pay for is art.

Yes, and janitors were *custodial engineers*.

Ninjutsu: the art of stealth, the art of invisibility.
Incredibly, books were actually being written on
the art of exceptional killing, on insidious, ignomini-
ous death, on murder as an art. Brett considered
opening a museum of murder. What a great idea.

Sudden puffs of steam fogged his vision. Tears
were streaming from his eyes, seeping under the
edge of his plastic goggles, and dropping onto the
white-hot metal.

He couldn't remember her name, couldn't remember his wife's name. She had been pregnant

when raped and murdered, and he couldn't remember her name.

He couldn't remember his parents' names. He couldn't remember his own name, either. The original one, before Brett Wallace.

Their names were gone, as were their faces. A vague shape filled his mind whenever he thought of her. An indistinct image. A feeling, mostly. A feeling of a happiness and contentment that could not possibly exist.

It had grown during the years of his wading through death. He had only been killing in earnest for three years: thirty-six months of almost nonstop killing. And during that time, his fading memory of *what's-her-name* grew to gigantic proportions in his subconscious. It grew until its pleasure turned to torturing pain.

Now she did not have a face. Now he couldn't remember what she was called.

He cried for himself. He cried for his lost life. He cried for his beautiful dead wife, the one whose name he couldn't remember.

The dead man cried. And kept working.

Hama had the sword. Rhea had the gun. Archer had nothing.

They entered the Dawn Dojo carefully, certain that Brett would be waiting for them. He had to know that they would discover the cause of Ambodini's death by now. And he had to know that they simply wouldn't hang around doing nothing about it.

Jeff walked across the wooden floor of the martial arts school. It was *his* school, and he was the single member of the trio unarmed. At least, he had no weapon other than his own skill—the skill Brett had taught him. If Brett was intent on fighting them, then he would face his student, his *deshi*, first.

Hama came next, his sword sheathed on his back. Rhea was just behind him, the dark 9mm silenced automatic clutched in her elegant hand. If Brett would not agree to ritual suicide, she had to shoot him. She would shoot him once in the heart and Hama would behead him as he fell. They had agreed in the car on the way over. He was to die a respected warrior's death if at all possible.

A warrior's head must not touch the ground—not attached to his neck, at any rate. The reasons for this were many and varied. The truth of the matter has been lost in antiquity, along with the ninjas' honor. Like it, the reason exists in the mind of each one who ponders it.

To discuss Brett's death in those calm terms was strange to Archer—downright weird and unnatural. They sat in the car and conversed about the proper way Wallace should die. But the man's existence and capabilities were undeniable. He did live to kill. He had killed many times, and with consummate skill. He was a dangerous man, more so now that he was threatening to lose control completely.

The dojo was empty. Archer moved to the cellar steps.

Hama stopped him. "No," he said, almost below Archer's hearing. "I will ... I *must* go first. If he is waiting ..."

Hama did not hesitate for an answer. Both orientals slipped by Archer and down the stairs. Hama knew the proper protocol: as Brett's executioner, he should face the Ninja Master first. *Deshis* be damned.

The door at the bottom was locked from the inside. Rhea leaned forward and expertly shot the bolt off. A split second later Hama kicked it open.

Light from upstairs spilled into the darkened enclosure. Rhea moved to the right, Archer to the left. Hama strode forward, his sword out, held over his head in both hands—the *Jodan no kamae* position. The light from upstairs silhouetted him, casting his shadow across the room.

Standing before them near the back wall, on the platform of knives, was a ninja.

The figure was covered from head to toe in black. His hands were covered. Even his eyes were covered—not by cloth, but by thin black glass goggles that were held to his head by a black elastic strap.

He stood casually, arms just away from his sides.

No one moved for fifteen seconds. In that fifteen seconds they all saw that the basement training area was a shambles. Targets had been torn from walls, mats had been gutted, weapons had been broken. The place was devastated. Not a single implement or device was left whole. It was as if

Brett were trying to destroy all connections he had to *ninjutsu*.

"*Jonin!*" Hama roared. "You have shamed your house, your fellows, your school! You have threatened the security of your clan!"

The figure in black did not reply. He did not move.

"You have threatened your heritage! Speak!"

The figure in black did not. Instead, it very slowly raised one leg and extended both arms. It stood on the platform on one foot, the left knee bent to the chest. The right arm was forward and slightly down. The left arm was up and back. The hands were at eighty-degree angles from the wrists.

Archer stared in wonder. "White crane," he breathed The man was in the preliminary stance of the white crane defensive style of martial arts.

Hama moved back. Both Rhea and Archer moved forward until they stood four feet from each other in a rough triangle.

"White crane," Jeff repeated. "'One hand lies, the other tells the truth.'" He took that right out of the manual.

"Defensive," Hama translated for himself, remembering. "He will not attack."

"But it is a deadly form if attacked," Rhea reminded both of them. "One hand is a diversion, the other a killing blow."

"But it's fucking Chinese," Archer concluded in wonder. "It's a specific Chinese kungfu style."

Hama moved forward, but not before Archer heard him. "If you were to fight two Japanese, what would you use?"

Hama moved forward until his shadow crossed the figure in black. He quickly sidestepped so the light was not blocked. The figure all but disappeared in Hama's shadow.

"You don't have to worry if you speak," Archer called to him. "We came to talk."

The figure said nothing. Archer didn't like the way this was going at all. Brett was set to fight. He was in uniform. He had even closed off his eyes. He was ready to take advantage of the darkness to escape . . . or kill.

"Brett, please!" Rhea cried. She held the gun up in both hands. "Please don't do this to us."

"No talk!" Hama bellowed. "No pleading! No further shame!"

Jeff walked quickly forward, not fast enough to threaten Brett, but fast enough to avoid being stopped by Hama. The man didn't even attempt to stop him.

"Talk to me," he begged. "You can't shut us out. You can't turn your back on the ninja. You know what will happen, what *is* happening. Explain, please, or you'll be wasting your life. All of your work will be meaningless. Even if you get away from us. Even if you kill us, the ninja will not rest. You'll have to face all of them."

The figure waited. In a defensive position.

Archer went for him.

He took two quick steps forward and leaped.

The figure jumped back and kicked the platform to meet him.

The movements were extremely powerful. Jeff's

jump took him eight feet off the floor. His arms were out and his legs bent to his waist. The figure's kick was short and devastating. It catapulted the knife-ridden platform into the air, the blades going right for Archer. The sound of the kick echoed in the room.

It was displaced by the sound Jeff's arms made shooting forward. His hands smashed into the platform floor, between knives. It knocked the platform back and up. Archer kicked down, again missing the knives. That knocked the platform back to the floor. Archer landed on it, dove sideways, and threw his legs over his head. He landed on his feet.

An arm shot out of the shadows. A hand in the position of a white crane beak smashed into Archer's chest. Archer was driven back, hard. He lost his footing. He fell heavily to the floor.

Hama stepped forward. The figure stepped back, out of the light. It was as if he disappeared. There was no puff of smoke. He simply became part of the darkness.

Rhea was crying as she pulled the gun's trigger twice. It coughed, and the sound of two ricochets off the opposite concrete wall followed.

"Turn on the lights!" Hama commanded, ripping off his black ninja hood and cocking his head. He stood, almost on his toes, his head averted, his eyes closed. He couldn't see the attack, so he *listened* for it.

Rhea ran for the lights. A whirlwind came out of the dark behind her. Fists crashed into her back, her kidney, and her neck. The punches came in rapid succession, driving her off her feet and into the wall. Her trigger finger was nearly broken when her gun hand slammed between the concrete and her body.

She cried out, a sound of pain, surprise, and girlish terror. A leg swept across her shoulders. The side of a black-garbed foot slammed into the side of her head. She was driven across the wall, the gun falling from her wounded fingers.

Archer was stunned. His addled brain rattled off the styles he saw from the floor, flat on his back. Brett had attacked Rhea with the *Choy-Li-Fut* style, a vicious spinning of fists. Archer tried to get up. A sudden stabbing pain where he had been hit forced him back for a second. The man's fingers had been like sharpened wooden stakes.

Brett's style changed like running water. From white crane to *Choy-Li-Fut* to *Pa Kwa*, the openhanded, sweeping, circular style he had kicked the woman with. Still in it, he spun to face Hama.

Hands against sword. The swinging *Pa Kwa* style was perfect. Hama slashed the air in brutal succession, never stopping, driving Brett back. Brett's hands windmilled, seemingly blocking, averting, then following Hama's slashes.

Archer wanted to tell the bald man to stop testing, stop feinting, attack! But he already knew that was what Hama was doing. Brett's skill only made it look as if Hama were purposely missing.

Archer catapulted to his feet. He ran toward the wall where Rhea and the light switch lay. Fighting

Brett in the darkened room was like fighting the wind or shadows. He lost substance with every move. His garb blended in with the gloom.

Brett backed Hama into the dark. Hama's eyes were still accustomed to the light. Brett suddenly switched styles again. The attack of the praying mantis. His arms became swords, his fingers blades, his feet wheels. Hama felt paralyzing stings across his own arms. His grip weakened.

Hama slashed once in desperation, violently to the side, and threw his body backward. He twisted in air, threw his arms wide, and somersaulted back into the light. He landed on his feet. The figure in black stepped forward and planted a straight-leg kick into Hama's side.

The swordsman was hurled back into the darkness. He fell heavily on his knees and hands. The sword spun away from him.

Archer dove over the fallen Japanese and somersaulted. He came up in a crouch, shielding Rhea's fallen body. She lay half on the floor and half on the wall as if she were caressing it. Archer had just a flash of image. It was her face. Her lips were split. Her nose was bleeding. Her eyes were closed. Her mouth worked. He spun on his toes, still crouched, and instantly defended.

Brett attacked with the low, slashing *Hung Gar* style. His stance was wide, and the open hand with its bent fingers sought to break bone, tear skin. If Jeff had let the blows through, Brett could have ripped his jaw from his face or broken Rhea's neck like a bamboo stalk.

Archer screeched and babbled, his own arms moving like lightning, his own hands slapping and pushing the blows away, monkey style.

Fight fire with fire, Brett had taught him. Fight Chinese style with Chinese style.

There are five monkey styles. Archer had no choice. He had to use "lost monkey." He slapped away Brett's blows while driving forward in a crouch. He slapped and rolled, pushing his opponent away. Suddenly the deflections were peppered with attacks. His curled hands bit at the figure. It was like pecking brick.

But he was far enough away from Rhea now. Lost monkey became wooden monkey, the attacker. No more rolls, no more slapping. Archer dove at the shadow, his hands shooting forward one after another, his legs twisting, spinning. Brett was driven back.

Archer looked for an opening. He looked desperately for a weakness in Brett's defense. To his growing horror, he couldn't find one. He was locked in a deadly fight with his teacher, his master, his mentor. It was not a fight where he could cry uncle.

Archer suddenly got "mindlock." He couldn't think. His monkey style was still functioning, but it was not fluctuating. His opponent instantly adjusted to the pattern of Archer's attack. Without unpredictability, he was doomed. Brett could adjust to his style and rip the monkey to pieces.

Archer saw it coming in despair: tiger claw. It tore the monkey paws down, it slashed across Jeff's flesh. It literally tore his shirt and ripped into his arms and chest. A claw went across his face. Four red lines decorated his cheek like Indian war paint.

His head was knocked sideways. He saw only the empty room. This was the moment: the tiger claw would become the crane beak. It would dive through his arms to his sternum. It would rupture his heart. Archer felt it coming.

Archer heard the sword. He never saw it.

Hama moved in, slicing. It wasn't a chopping style as before, it was a thrusting technique. The blade snaked between the fighters and slashed out at Brett.

He was forced to move back. Quickly. Hama kept driving him back, spinning and slicing at him with the sword. Hama backed him to the wall. Brett raced toward it. Hama followed, trying to push the incredibly sharp blade through the deflecting arms, into the trunk, between the ribs and into the blackened, corrupt heart.

Hama was certain from Brett's speed and manner that the man meant to bounce from the wall, leaping over him. There he would deliver a blow to the top of Hama's skull or the back of his neck, severing the spine from the brain. Hama would be ready. His sword would rise, cutting Brett open as he flew backward, upside down, over him.

They neared the wall. Hama planted his feet. His sword arced up.

The figure in black dropped.

He dropped, his leg shooting out, his foot connecting with Hama's knee.

Hama tipped and crumpled to the floor, his face twisted in pain. Brett's forearm smashed across the tortured visage. Archer heard the crack from across the room. Hama slammed to the floor like a dynamited tree trunk.

A figure swept by Archer. Rhea had run forward. Brett snatched the sword from Hama's limp hands. He held it by his side, ready to cut Rhea down as she approached him. She stopped ten feet away from him and raised the gun she clutched in her shaking hands.

Archer could foretell the outcome. Brett would weave with the darkness. Rhea would miss. He would move in and slice her across the chest, through the heart. She would die. He would drive the blade into Hama's eye, to his brain. He would die.

There would only be Brett and Archer left. Jeff could not beat him. He would die.

There was only one way to prevent it. If Rhea could see Brett clearly, she could shoot him. He would die.

Jeff's fingers sought out the light switch. He flicked it up.

For a split second the room was sharply illuminated in bright white light.

Then the light bulb exploded, raining flaming napalm into the room.

4

It was an old trick, made popular by the movies. That's where Jeff Archer had seen it before. Napalm was injected into a light bulb; when electric current reached it, it exploded.

In a small, enclosed area like a jail cell or a bathroom, it was deadly and horrid. In the huge training area, it was bad enough. Flaming, undulating balls of fire splashed down and slammed to the floor, reacting like liquid fire; it spread.

The figure in black moved back easily. He knew it had been coming. Rhea was hurled to the floor when a gob hit her in the back. Hama tried to regain full consciousness, rolling away.

Archer had cringed, his arms covering his face. The stench almost overwhelmed him. The room immediately filled with choking, deadly smoke.

But there was only one way out. That was the door Archer was blocking. He straightened, coughing, waiting for the inevitable attack.

He waited for thirty seconds. He nearly panicked twice in that time. His mind screamed at him to run, but he couldn't leave Rhea and Hama. And he couldn't go to them—rescue them—because that would leave the door unguarded. Brett could escape *and* trap them inside.

After what Archer had seen, he didn't know which was worse: dying in the inferno or allowing Brett loose on the city. He held his ground.

When the attack came, it was true to form—the unexpected. The figure in black did not go for the door, he went for Rhea. She rolled, panic-stricken, on the ground, trying to put out the flames on her back while avoiding the others.

Archer screamed at her. The napalm couldn't be doused. It would eat through her shirt in a matter of seconds and spread across her skin like Krazy Glue.

She finally tore off her shirt and threw it to the ground. All she wore then was a bra and her jeans. Brett came at her from the side, the sword held back like an archer's string.

She countered his first thrust and attacked, her leg slashing the air. He merely hopped to the side behind her and swung the sword again to chop her in half. She had to leap over the blade, trying to kick him again in midair. He moved his head back. She missed. When she landed, the sword was waiting for her.

He slashed at her ankles. She had to dive back to avoid the blow. He slashed at her heart to keep her off balance. There was no way she could remain on her feet. She fell onto her back.

Archer ran forward. Suddenly there was a vial in Brett's hand. He threw it at Jeff. Archer's attack became a retreat. The vial hit the floor, broke, and more flame spread. Its sudden conflagration cleared the smoke for just a second. Archer could see the scene clearly.

Rhea was on her back to one side. Hama was moving feebly on his back to the other side. Between them, in easy slicing range, was Brett Wallace. He stood ceremoniously between them, the sword held before him in two hands: the *Chudan no kamae* position. He would slash downward one way and then the other. Rhea and Hama would be torn from the crotch to the neck. Archer could not get to them.

Still, he would die trying. He ran toward the wall of blocking flame as the figure in black began to move his sword.

Something smashed into Archer's shoulder, forcing him down, rooting him to the spot. Something catapulted above the flames, having used Archer as a step. Something rammed something else forward, catching the figure in black squarely in the chest, knocking him back. Something landed where the figure had been, something in black with no hood.

The something turned around. That something was Brett Wallace.

Archer reeled back from the smoke and the heat. The figure in black, their attacker, had not been the Ninja Master.

Then who the fuck was it?

Archer only had time for the question. He ran back to the wall and up the stairs. He grabbed the first mat he could get his hands on and almost fell back down the stairs again. He threw it like a net, over the wall of flame blocking him. It made a temporary bridge between him and his fellows. He ran forward as Brett spun the dark brown wooden staff in his hands, driving back the attacker.

Archer had never seen the stick before. It was more than five feet long and imperfect, as if made from a tree limb. But Brett used it as if it were part of his body. His style was assured and seamless. It did not allow the attacker to slip the sword through. Brett spun the staff, jabbed, cut, and swung. The attacker was driven back into the flames.

Archer bundled Rhea into his arms and started toward the stairs. To his astonishment, the attacker stood amid the flames, still fighting. The black suit . . . the suit had to be flame-resistant. Or they were fighting a zombie.

Brett was indifferent. It did not have the bodyguard's face, so he would fight it. The battle was incredibly fast and precise. To Archer's eyes, it seemed as if the two were mirror images. There didn't seem to be any move and countermove. They seemed to do things at the exact same time. There didn't look to be any question as to which offensives or defenses each would use. It was almost ballet. It was choreographed dance, a dance of death.

Suddenly Brett changed his tactic. He slammed the stick-tip down and did a standing pole vault over the attacker. Before the man could bring the sword up, Brett dropped on him amid the flames.

That was all Archer saw of the fight. Then both men fell back into the fire. Archer ran up the stairs and dropped Rhea on the dojo mats. He was at the cellar door by the time Hama had crawled halfway up the steps. Archer raced to him, grabbed a handful of his tunic, and dragged him the rest of the way. The orientals helped each other out to the street. Archer leaped back to the basement. He landed on his knees before the open doorway.

The heat was numbing. The smoke was blinding and choking. Archer couldn't get back into the room. He was forced up the steps. He fell at the summit, trying to breathe.

Brett almost broke the man's wrist. The attacker slipped his arm from Brett's grip just before the bone cracked. But it was enough to make him drop the *ninja-to*. Brett pulled down, his feet finding the oven-hot floor. His hands dove in, through the attacker's awkward, unprepared defense.

He got the man's head. At the least, he would tear the mask and visor from the man's face. At the medium, he would break the man's neck. At the most, he would tear the man's head off.

All the man did was touch Brett's wrist.

Brett's arms were paralyzed. A hacksaw tore through his shoulders. His heart stopped for a second. He fell back into the fire.

The figure in black had an extra color. Something golden flashed between his forefinger and thumb. A needle.

Jeff had to be dragged out by the firemen. The street was filled with trucks and ambulances. The buildings on either side were being evacuated. Flashing red and blue lights mingled with the streetlamps to bathe the area in disco colors. Thick beige hoses were everywhere. Men in white, yellow, and black raced from place to place.

Archer was dragged to the pavement and pulled onto a stretcher. Hands tore open his shirt, pushed a rubber oxygen mask over his mouth, and strapped his legs down. He had to be taken to the hospital and treated for smoke inhalation, he heard someone say. Then his arms started moving.

One intern was hurled over the stretcher. Another was kicked back. Archer bounced off the stretcher as if it were a trampoline. He vaulted over the medicos and pushed his way through the firefighters. He clawed his way to the front of the mob.

The water had no effect on the napalm. Archer stared in disbelief as the Dawn Dojo burned to the ground.

Little Tiger Williams was in heaven.
Today he was big enough. For years Daddy had

been putting him off, saying, "Someday, when
you're big enough."

Today was the day.

Daddy took him into town. In the coming years,
he would argue with his father; their opinions
would differ; they would grow cold toward each
other. But he would always complete the Sunday
ritual.

Today was the day. Today the ritual was born.

His father put him in the front seat of the
station wagon. The front seat, next to him, Not the
backseat, where the kids go. Not the backseat,
where Bart wanted to sit.

Tiger's heart sank when Bart started whining
about "Why can't I come too?" and "It's not fair!"
But Dad had only let Tiger go. Bart wasn't old
enough.

"Someday when you're big enough," Tiger had
told his little brother.

Bart had burst into tears and run into his room.

Bart would never be big enough. Bart would
drown in a lake at summer camp. Daddy would
sue the camp and win a lot of money, but it
wouldn't bring Bart back. But that was years from
now.

Today was the day. The Day of the Ritual. They
drove into town, side by side. They drove into
Chinatown where the air was thick with the stench
of gunpowder and the streets were carpeted in
streams of yellow and red. It was the Year of the
Rabbit. It was the New Year celebration.

Firecrackers went off every few seconds. And

not Kansas firecrackers. Not even Ohio cherry bombs. These were Chinese firecrackers: big, round tubes on strings that would burst, then burst again and again, and again, rapid-fire. Boom! Then bang-bang-bang-bang-bang! Then again, boombangbangbangbangbang, over and over.

And every time they burst, they'd leave tatters of red and yellow packing. Tiger slid through it like kicking through fallen autumn leaves. Dad might wince at the explosions once in a while, but not Tiger. It was a miracle to him. It was indescribably wonderful. Words like exotic and fascinating would come to him years later.

Heaven wasn't enough. Dad took him to nirvana. On a street bend, there was a little shop, its windows clouded by fog that came from inside. Tiger could only see the strange red slashing symbols in the window. Chinese characters, Chinese letters, Chinese words.

Dad opened the door for him and ushered him inside. He walked into a haze of misting candy. The air was so thick with wonderful smells it nearly knocked him back. The glass display case was bigger than he was. It was filled with things Tiger had never seen before. Dripping things, puffy things, browned circular things, wiggly things, wobbling white things.

Daddy pointed at many different things and told the counterman how many of each he wanted. Tiger held out his arms for two big white boxes tied with string. Daddy carried two big bags; one murky wax paper, the other brown and opaque.

They walked back to the festive streets and stopped at another store. Tiger stood among legs, sniffing the delicious boxes. In his nose was the pastry smell. In his ears was amazing chatter, like monkeys laughing.

When they got back to the car Daddy had a thick newspaper under his arm. They drove back to the house, Tiger actually bouncing on the seat with excitement. All was forgiven when Bart saw the bags and boxes. He knew what they meant. Sweets, dessert, cakes, cookies, pastries. The boys tore into them as though it were Christmas.

Mom frowned, but Daddy's laughter soon won her over. They shared the morning with delight— real, actual, honest delight. Tiger tasted things he had never tasted before. Creme buns. Flaky pastry covered in dripping honey. Jellied foam. He and Bart would ooh and ahh and ick through the food as Mommy and Daddy laughed, sipped their rich coffee, and read their paper.

They were a family. They loved.

Brett Wallace laughed and laughed and laughed. Love. He felt it. He couldn't control it. It was nowhere in his head. It was in his heart. It was so excruciatingly wonderful, it practically tore at his heart. He knew what the songs meant now. His heart was so full, it felt it would burst. He wished it would. Because way back in his mind, he knew what had to happen next.

Way, way back in his head was screaming. If he ran toward the sound, he'd see a person far in the distance screaming. If he kept running, he'd recognize the person. And when he wanted to stop, he wouldn't be able to. He'd be pulled right to the person. He would be dragged until he was staring right into the person's screaming face.

Brett Wallace was screaming. Brian "Tiger" Williams was screaming.

Brett tried to laugh over the scream. He laughed so hard his mouth hurt. He turned to look at his brother. His brother was dead, drowned. His brother's eyes bulged, his tongue stuck out of his open mouth, and his skin was green.

Brett turned to his parents, his laughter shrieking. He couldn't see them anymore. Parts of them were lying on the floor, against the wall, on the furniture. They had been ripped apart. Their blood had been splattered on the walls as words.

That was not the worst.

In the middle of the room, there was something Brett didn't know. But he recognized it. He never saw it before, but he knew what it was. It was a tiny little thing, beautiful in its perfection.

It was Brian Williams' child. It was the baby his wife Kyoko had given him.

It was small and beautiful and perfect. And it was dead.

"KYOKO!"

Brett Williams screamed the name again and again. He kept screaming until his voice was a hoarse, dreadful whisper.

Rhea sat on the bed and held him in her arms as

tightly as she ever held anything. She cried while he screamed, her racking sobs almost as violent as his waking nightmare.

She rocked him when he stopped, but she couldn't stop crying. She cried aloud as he whispered to her.

She moved her torso back and forth, holding him. His arms were lightly around her back. He did not know where he was or who she was. He did not know who he was.

They sat up on the bed, holding each other. Rhea couldn't stop crying as Brett repeated the same words endlessly.

"*Kyoko*. That was my wife's name."

5

The Rhea Dawn was a fortress, closed to the public. The staff had been fired. The ovens had been shut down. The front door had been locked and barred.

"We should kill him now," Hama said miserably.

"Just wait long enough!" Rhea lashed out at him. "The poison and the fever will do it for you!"

Hama sighed. He explained it carefully, almost reluctantly, as he had a half-dozen times before.

"The instructions from the *Hanshi* were explicit. He can no longer be trusted."

"The person we attacked was not Brett!" Archer stressed again, also for the seventh time. "He could have been framed."

"I explained that situation very carefully to the *Hanshi*." Hama said the next words gravely,

distrustfully. "I took your word for what happened."
Hama had been nearly unconscious when Brett
appeared.

"I can understand you not believing me," Archer snapped. "I almost expect it. But Rhea backs
me up on this!"

Hama looked at the woman with a tinge of
disgust. "She is in love," he said flatly.

She looked back at him with equal abhorrence.
"I would not lie, Yamabushi," she told him coldly.

"So *you* say."

"That's enough!" Archer shouted.

"It makes no difference," Hama continued. "It
doesn't change Wallace's manner before the fight.
The *Hanshi* maintains that there is more to it than
simply his actions here. There are other things
that throw doubt upon his loyalty."

"I'd like to hear what they are!" Rhea countered.

"The *Hanshi* did not say," Hama told her carefully.
"The *Hanshi* does not *have* to say."

Archer kept his equilibrium, but just barely.
The changes that had occurred in the last five
hours had altered his entire perception of the last
five years.

There was only one exit from the dojo training
cellar that Jeff knew of. There was obviously another that Brett knew. When they had finally
gotten back to the restaurant, they had found the
Ninja Master facedown on his bed.

Hama had contacted the *Hanshi*, the Master, in
Japan. For some unnamed reason, the ninja *ryu*
had come to disfavor Brett Wallace. The standing

order had remained: eliminate and disband the Wallace *ryu*. Rhea was to return to Japan. Hama and Rhea were to decide what to do with Archer.

Suddenly, Hama was no longer *genin*/operative. He was a *yamabushi*, a warrior-priest. He was a descendant of a group of mountain monks who sometimes aided, and sometimes lorded over, ninja families. He, like the monks before him, was a watcher, a judge, and when he had to be, a jury and executioner. He, like them, made decisions based on the good of all, not just the partisan desires of a warlord, shogun, or emperor.

Archer did not have to speak, for Hama's reluctance to carry out the orders was already obvious. Brett was still alive. But Archer wanted to speak. He needed to.

"The *Hanshi* is not God," he pleaded. "He could have been fooled the way we had been fooled."

"Be careful, Genin," Hama warned. "You assume too much."

"Fact," Jeff countered. "Brett saved all our lives at The Revenge House. Fact: the experience changed him. Fact: he was more secretive, but there was no clear evidence that he was becoming destructive or careless. Fact: Carlo Ambodini was murdered, but no evidence points conclusively to Brett. Fact: *someone else* was in the dojo and tried to kill us.

"Fact. Brett saved our lives. Again."

Hama held his hand up. "Enough." He nodded slowly. "I will wait until Wallace is conscious. I will wait until he can respond to the charges against him."

"If he ever regains consciousness," Rhea said bitterly.

She moved to the stairs. Neither Hama nor Archer made any move to question or stop her. She retrieved the bowl of herbal water and the washcloth in the loft. She rejoined Brett by his bedside and cleansed the perspiration from his brow and chest. She moistened the cloth with the herbs and dripped it onto his parched lips.

The *yamabushi* and *genin* waited in silence. The former, for the Ninja Master to regain awareness; the latter, for a renewed attack of the figure in black.

It was only common sense, Archer reasoned. He had been toying with them at the dojo. It was obvious to Jeff that he was skilled enough to kill them all before Brett arrived. But, he supposed, the figure wanted their deaths to look like an accident. Why else booby-trap the light bulb?

It was the only theory that made any sense. The figure had planted the napalm to kill Brett or his ninja *genin*, but was caught in the act by the *genin* trio. Then, in his egotistic bravado, he sparred with them, knowing the light would be turned on to fight him. He too must have known of the secret second exit. He was too assured not to.

But now the *genin* and *jonin* were still alive, and all knew of the figure's presence. It only made sense that he would attack again. But how? Instead of napalm and kungfu, would it be plastique and assault rifles? Archer could only wait and see.

He did not have long to wait.

Rhea screamed both their names. They heard an explosion. The building shook, and fire belched down the stairs like the devil's tongue.

The men tumbled into the kitchen. Hama grabbed the fire extinguisher and Jeff grabbed the ax, then both charged the flaming stairs. Hama sprayed the white foam as he went. He stamped up the stairs, Jeff right behind him.

The flames were worse at the balcony. This time Hama emptied the extinguisher without creating a path. Together the men hacked at the balcony's ceiling, the loft's floor. Archer's ax broke through and Hama tore open a makeshift trapdoor with his bare hands.

Hama pounded through, jumping to the left. Archer leaped and pulled himself through to the right.

The opening to the outside—what used to be French doors to the left of the sleeping area—was framed in flames. Another firebomb had been hurled at the stairs to prevent the men's entrance. Rhea danced with the figure in black.

Through the haze, it looked as if they were doing a particularly violent series of sign languages. But she was fighting with her karate and jujitsu training while he was battering her with *Wing Chun*, the short, explosive stabs of the fist and fingers.

"Chinese," Hama barked with hate.

The figure's head didn't move, but a "snake fist" spun through Rhea's attack and knocked her back.

He pivoted, and his arm swung toward the men as if he were pitching a softball.

Instead, something shiny and glowing stretched from his hand. It twisted in the air and bit at Archer's face. The bite became a sting which became a punch and then a stunning blow. Jeff reeled back, his jaw cut open by the metal whip.

It was a linked series of small, thin metal bones. It had a pointed flyweight at the tip. Used correctly, it could go through a man or tear him to shreds.

Hama dove forward, grabbing for the steel snake. The figure was too fast. The whip sped back to him and then lashed out again, this time directly at Hama.

Rhea kicked it in the middle in midflight. It bent, missing Hama. He ducked under it and came at the figure. Jeff hefted the ax in his hands and wished he had Rhea's gun. He held the hatchet across his torso and charged.

The figure hurled the whip behind him, and in the same motion brought Hama's sword from the *saya* on his back. The Japanese man slammed his feet to the wooden floor and froze in a defiant karate stance. He would counter his own sword's blows with his chopping arms. The *ninja-to* slashed and spun, the figure sidling forward. Hama shifted back, surprisingly nimble for such a burly man.

Rhea moved in, trying to collapse the figure's ribs from the side. He suddenly swept down low in an elegant Tai Chi Chuan split. It looked slow, but the leg that swept back toward the woman was anything but that. The figure spun in place, the sword always aimed at Hama, as his foot slammed Rhea's chin like an open palm.

Her own leg swept from under her and she dropped face first onto the bed. The figure was up already, slashing the sword fluidly in the *Sampo-Giri* style to back up Hama and deflect Archer's weapon.

Jeff sucked in his breath. The man's technique was perfect. His breathing was perfect. He was totally in command. He was still toying with them, utilizing an encyclopedic knowledge of both Chinese and Japanese martial art techniques. It was almost a farcical fight. Four people trying to kill each other in the mid-1980's using ancient battle arts. Four people amid a roaring inferno sparring with each other, utilizing the most precise and elegant movements.

Jeff swung the hatchet up, trying to use the pickax butt to puncture the figure's knee or calf. Archer had to hurl the ax to the side to deflect the metal whip which suddenly sprang from the figure's left hand. At the same time, the attacker twisted the *ninja-to* in to rip the front of Hama's tunic.

Hama knocked the blade aside with his forearm. Archer caught the whip around the ax head and held it tight. Both men moved in. The figure vaulted in the air—as if the floorboards were a trampoline—and kicked at both.

Hama blocked the blow with his other arm. Archer rolled out of the way. He wound up in a crouch, yanking at the hatchet, ripping the metal whip from the figure's hand.

The figure was not going to lose it without a fight. He hurled the other end at Archer. It snapped across Jeff's torso, knocking him to his back. The metal bones twisted through his shirt and into his chest, ripping hair and flesh. He scraped across the floor in pain, his head hitting the table leg.

Hama and Rhea stood side by side, facing the figure, blocking him from the bed. He ran at them, the sword forward. Hama and Rhea moved as two parts of a single fighting machine. They should have known better. The man was making it too easy. He was practically begging them to capture the blade and wrest it from his grip.

Which is exactly what they did. They moved away from each other, one on each side of the thrusting blade, then reunited, locking the sword in their judo grips and trying to tear it from the attacker's hands with all their combined strength.

The sword came out of his fingers with no effort. The man threw it at them. They were off balance for a split second. In that second the man pushed his hands at their faces. Stinging, blinding powder erupted from his wrists. It smacked the orientals full in the face.

The powder clung to their skin, burned their eyes, and stuffed their nostrils. They reeled back, their sense of balance gone. The figure merely moved between them, nonchalantly reclaiming the *ninja-to* from their useless fingers.

He moved right to the bed and pulled the sword up in the overhead *Jodan no kamae* position.

"*Menq her huah fen!*" the figure shrieked. "*Menq her poh huay!*"

He brought the sword down across Brett's stomach.

Sparks sizzled across the bedspread as the blade collided with the blocking ax.

The figure stood on one side; Archer stood on the other. They battled over Brett's body. The attacker cut and slashed with the sword fluidly, trying to break Archer's jabbing, twisting defense. The hatchet was like a mutating tool in Jeff's hands. He was fighting for his *sensei*'s life, he was fighting for *his Hanshi*'s honor. His Master gave him the power and the skill he needed.

But it was not enough. The figure seemed to tire of testing the *ryu*'s mettle and determination. The sword suddenly pulled back as Jeff swung the ax down to block a feint. He nearly buried the hatchet blade in Brett's chest. He fought the downward thrust. It was then the figure stepped forward and punched him hard in the face.

Archer fell back, his nose broken. The figure spun the sword up as he jumped on the bed, his feet on either side of Brett's body.

"*Menq her maan chi!*" he cried and drove the sword tip toward Brett Wallace's chest.

The dead man rejoined his wife in Japan.

Brian and Kyoko stood side by side on the coast of Katsuura, just across the peninsula from Chiba. It was Williams' true home, not San Francisco. He was with his true love in his true home, letting the beauty and serenity wash over him like waves.

The darkness appeared but it did not. The shadow was there but it was not. Kyoko stood by him but she did not. Without seeing it, Williams knew the darkness was descending. The shadow grew across the land but it did not move. Kyoko stood, but was somewhere else, in a different dimension, on a different plane.

The closest he could come to rationally understanding it was as a living double exposure.

He felt it with certainty in the part of the brain that cannot be explained. He looked into his friends' faces. They hung in his mind like prized paintings. He walked through a wide-open, gray, light-infused hallway where Rhea, Hama, and Archer stood.

"Menq her huah fen," said one

"Menq her poh huay," said another.

"Menq her maan chi," said the third.

His friends' faces were his enemy's, but they did not change.

A man laughed, far away. Williams followed the sound. He walked across the world. It brought him to a room without walls or ceiling. It was a room without floors, but it was a room, still.

A man who is there but is not, laughs but does not. Williams does not see him there, but has knowledge of him there. He does not see the face but he knows it. All he sees is the insect.

Copper plating on its back. A horrible, moving face. Two long, pincerlike antennae. Four skittering legs. It changes.

It is a dragon. Head of a camel, horns of a deer, eyes of a monster, ears of a steer, neck of a serpent, stomach of a clam, scales of a fish, paws of a tiger, claws of an eagle.

A dragon which laughs.

The face of his friends, his enemies, the man, the insect, the dragon . . . laughs. Then dissolve in fire.

Brett Wallace's eyes snapped open. His hands slapped together over his chest.

The *ninja-to* was locked between his palms, the blade tip touching his chest.

Brett lashed out with a leg, sweeping the figure from the bed as if harvested. The man slammed onto the floor on his back and slid across the room into the electronics-covered bookshelves.

The bookcases rocked, ever so slowly, then started to topple over like a last, lazy nudged tenpin. The shelves crashed onto the figure, bursting with a renewed flash of flame.

Brett Wallace stood on the bed, the sword in one hand, a pair of black string-tied pants around his waist.

His life burned around him. Everything he had built, everything he had depended upon, all his tools, were destroyed. Fire had consumed everything. The computer, with its links to police and government reports. The clothes, the uniforms, the costumes of infiltration. The weapons, both ancient and modern. The home—*his* home.

The life of Brett Wallace was now over, con-

sumed in fire. Nothing the Ninja Master had
started with existed now.

It made no difference. Brett Wallace didn't know
his name. The fever had wiped it from his mind.
But he remembered what he was. He knew his
destiny. He was reborn in the flames.

Brian Williams slammed the sword through the
bed, into the floor. He came off the bed and ran
toward the contorting figures of Rhea and Hama.
He threw the woman over his shoulder and dragged
Hama by the scruff of his neck, holding both the
man's shirt and skin. He carried them through the
door's circle of flame to the building's roof. They
rolled there, gasping and clawing at their eyes.

The Ninja Master instantly dove back into the
inferno to find Archer. The wounded *genin* was
trying to sit up inside the bathroom. Blood streamed
from his nose and chin, and his chest had been
badly slashed. He was mumbling incoherently.
Something about failing his *Hanshi*. Williams gently
took him by the shoulders and pulled him toward
the door.

The bookcases exploded upward. The figure in
black hurled the smoldering oak and pine from
him. He kicked the furniture aside with vigorous
strength. He surveyed the room like a caged
lion until seeing Williams. Then he slowed and
straightened. The figure in black stood, waiting.

Williams stared in confusion at the figure. How
was he supposed to understand this? He wakes up
from a nightmare in a strange place. People he
knows but does not recognize lie across a burning

floor, their faces and eyes ruined. A figure, a haunting figure, rises from flaming devastation to confront him.

Williams lowered the wounded young man to the floor and walked toward the figure. He would do what he had to until the figure told him the meaning of his torture, the reason for his attacks.

Archer was suddenly seized by a desperate need to stop his *sensei*. His mind was telling him something his brain couldn't understand. He clutched at Williams' legs as he passed. His weakened arms couldn't stop him completely, but they slowed the Ninja Master. He looked down irritably.

It was that moment the figure chose to charge.

With a surge of strength, Archer lurched up. He slammed the Ninja Master aside with his left arm. His right elbow swung and collided with his *sensei*'s jaw, knocking him away. He dove at the figure as the man's hand shot forward.

The second golden needle, like the first, was meant for the Ninja Master. Instead, it sank into Archer's left forearm.

With his right, Archer threw a killing blow. He had neither the skill nor the knowledge to deliver a death hand—the mythical strike that disrupted the life force—but he could kill. His fingers were steel, his arm iron. He rammed his hand at the figure's skull, directly next to the attacker's ear.

The covered head slipped to the side, almost imperceptibly. Archer's fingertips smashed into the figure's head. His feet slid on the floor as if it had suddenly become ice. He crouched, his arms jabbing. He took two steps back and dove sideways. His body landed heavily in the thickest part of the flames.

Williams tried to get to his feet. Archer moved over to aid him. The needle seemed to hum as soon as he tried to move. His nerves were pulled taut. They thickened and became stiff like dried leather. They choked off his circulation. He couldn't see for a second.

Suddenly screaming in agony, Archer pulled the needle from his arm.

The ceiling collapsed onto Archer and his *Hanshi*.

The Ninja Master got up. It was not easy, but he did it. He heard the firemen and the paramedics trying to dig through the left from the kitchen. Other than that, the room was silent. Outside—it was all outside now—the city moved on. Voices, vehicles, birds, insects. The moon was out. Its blue light mixed with the surrounding buildings' lights to give the scene of devastation a soft glow.

The Ninja Master looked down. Jeff Archer lay at his feet, facedown. His back moved slightly, rhythmically. He breathed. The Ninja Master looked to his right. Hama and Rhea lay still on the rubble from the ceiling. They breathed evenly as well. They had fainted, but would live.

The Ninja Master looked up. When the ceiling had collapsed, it had not only poured its plaster and insulation down but also unleashed the contents of the ruptured pipes. It had saved all their lives.

The Ninja Master looked to his left. No one else

was amid the devastation. Perhaps the collapsing ceiling had not fallen to their rescue after all. Perhaps someone else, someone who tried to kill them . . .

Brett cried again, for all his past lives. It wasn't a wrenching, horrible emotion. It was a simple feeling of loss. It was a ritual of honor, these new tears. The demon had been cleansed from him, but now it was loose upon the world.

There were no more nightmares. This was something tangible, something real, something mysterious, complex, and unspeakably inhuman. Something truly evil.

He had been prepared. The man walked away from the wreckage, leaving the sleeping bodies behind.

The Ninja Master was dead. Long live the Ninja Master.

PART TWO

"We classify disease as error, which nothing but Truth or Mind can heal."

Mary Baker Eddy

6

White.

Jeff Archer had on a single light.

The lone illumination made a pool on the tabletop. The white Formica of the surface reflected the light into Archer's eyes. That was bad, but not so bad as the entire room had been with all the lights on.

White walls, twelve feet high; white acoustically tiled ceilings; white tables with white plastic chairs; white lab coats; white dresses, white shoes, white hosiery; white curtains over white shades; white skin—it was more than a pleasure, it was a relief to look at the blue-green indoor/outdoor carpet stretched wall to wall.

Archer had had to turn off the overhead fluorescent lights. The reflection hurt his eyes. And what hurt his eyes also hurt his head. Instead, he had turned on the single desktop fixture on one of the room's six tables. He hunched over it, looking from one open book to another.

"*Meng her huah fen.*"

Meng . . . dream.

Her . . . and.

Huah . . .

Archer could not find the translation in the dictionary.

Fen . . .

Fen di was a cemetery. *Fen hong se* was pink. *Fen mo* was powder. *Feng* was the wind. *Feng kuang* was crazy.

You can say that again, Jeff thought.

Maybe not *huah fen*, he thought, trying again. Maybe *huah-fen*, or *huahfen*.

Huah fen . . . divide.

Dream and divide.

Men her poh huay. Or *poh-huay.* Or *pohhuay.*

Dream and destroy.

Meng her maan chi/maan-chi/maanchi.

Dream and . . . expire. Dream and die.

Archer closed the English-Chinese/Chinese-English paperback dictionary. He looked at the remaining open book.

"*Ninjutsu,*" he read, "the art of stealth. . . . Ninjas were generally considered spies; therefore, ninja assignments were generally those of infiltration, assassination, and sabotage."

Archer grimaced inwardly.

"In feudal Japanese wars, a ninja's responsibilities were as far-ranging as the battle strategies themselves. But rather than being the noble warriors that are portrayed in modern studies—the loyal subject fighting for the honor of Japan outside the restrictive Bushido code of samurai conduct—the ninja were actually ancient terrorists, members of a ninja 'family' available to anyone with the most gold."

Archer's arm shot out to the side, chopping an invisible, nonexistent antagonist, then returned to the tabletop.

"Although comparable to the Italian families of the Cosa Nostra, or Mafia, in the Northeast during the early twentieth century, ninjas could also be compared to present-day street gangs, in that most members were related either by blood or temperament and it wasn't unusual for the ninjas to plot an insurrection merely to gain control of more territory."

Archer shook his head minutely, as if "tsking." The vibration of his head became more pronounced, then stilled. He grimaced again.

"Rather than respected, the ninja were feared, from the moment of their creation (generally assumed to be approximately 500 A.D.) to their disbanding along with the samurai in the early 1900s. But in the fourteen centuries between, the ninja made a name for themselves—etched in infamy. Their legacy was one of chaos, anarchy, cruelty, and death."

Archer had seen enough for one night. He was going to close the book when a final sentence caught his eye. He slowly laid the pages before him.

"Their killings were not limited to their assignments," Archer read on. "To reveal any ninja secret to anyone outside the 'family' meant death at the hands of one's own group, as well as death to those told."

Archer slowly closed the book. He stared across the light into the darkness. Even if all the fluorescent bulbs above had been on, Archer would still have seen nothing but a figure in black, a figure who moved from kungfu style to kungfu style as if a creature formed from a dozen animals: claws of a tiger, beak of a crane, arms of a snake, legs of a mantis, head of a monkey.

He was a figure who moved from creature to creature with a constantly changing flow of movements and speeds: the fastball of *Wing Chun*, the curve of *Pa Kwa*, the slow ball of *Tai Chi Chuan*, and the screwball of *Choy-Li-Fut*. The game analogy played in Archer's head. Why not an automatic pistol or rifle? Why firebombs and steel whips? Why not a hitman's bullet from a football field away instead of a one-man assault on a loft headquarters?

Was it all a game? A game with death at every base?

There was little doubt in Jeff's mind that the figure would have pushed Hama's sword through Brett's body and into the bed if the Ninja Master hadn't stopped him. There used to be no doubt at all, but time had clouded his memory as if his brain had been smeared with petroleum jelly. After all, Archer hadn't come completely out of his delirium for two months. And then there had been another two months to fully recuperate from his wounds.

Only then did he start his physical therapy and the real tests, the tests that would determine whether he would ever fully recover, began. Now it was sixteen weeks later and he was still no closer to a logical answer about why the attack had come. Now, thirty-two weeks from the incident at the Rhea Dawn, it all seemed to be a particularly unpleasant and unbelievable occurrence. On sunny mornings, Jeff had to convince himself it all had actually happened. On overcast days, he had to tell himself it was not worse than it was.

In both cases, Archer was having a harder and harder time of it.

"So there you are." All the lights went on. Archer screwed his eyes shut against them and moaned.

"Oh God, I'm sorry." Half the lights went off. Then they started to come back on, and the other half went off. Then the fluorescents did a little dance until only a third were illuminated and they were in opposite sides of the room. Archer's area was comfortably gloomy.

"I'm really sorry, Jeff," the brown-haired woman said with sympathy as she approached the table. "Do you have a headache?"

Archer nodded wearily as the female in the

brown pants and lab coat went around the table and sat opposite him.

"What's this?" she asked, turning the thick hard-cover book around to face her. "*Secret Weapons*, by Geoffrey Merrick," she read. She opened the book and flipped through the chapters: "'The Axis' World War Two Secrets,' 'The Israeli Desert's Secret,' 'The Orient's Secret Army.' Sounds pretty secret."

"Not as secret as my condition." Archer's voice matched his expression—exhausted. "Are we going to talk, or are you just going to pump me for more blood and information?"

He instantly regretted his sarcasm. The look on her face seemed to cut through to "guilt central" in his brain. She had been the first thing he saw when he woke up in the hospital. She had been supervising his recovery ever since. It is said that a patient's love for his doctor is unavoidable—especially in long-term cases and very especially when the doctor is a pretty young woman.

A pretty, young, sensitive woman.

Archer didn't apologize. She swallowed her hurt instantly, like a true pro, and got down to cases. Through half-closed eyes, leaning back in his chair, his hands in his lap, Archer saw that she wore a very pretty light-colored print shirt under her coat. She had a nice figure, a nice face—long, with thin lips and bright green eyes—and she had a mole next to her nose.

Her hair was cut short, but she had paid enough attention to it to highlight the front with subtle blond streaks. A tiny tuft of blond hair also hung at the back of her neck. A "New Wave" doctor.

"No blood," she said lightly, "but more information."

Archer groaned and rolled his eyes.

"But not *from* you tonight," she continued brightly, "to you."

It took him a second to catch on. It was like that all the time now. Archer used to be pretty sharp. He could understand deductive as well as inductive reasoning. He got the punch lines to all kinds of jokes faster than the average person, and he caught on to esoteric concepts with ease.

It was like... it was as if ideas were living things that threw themselves at his brain. Eight months ago, they'd pass through his skull and into his mind with no problem. Now they were having to slam themselves against his head a few times before getting through.

She got up when she saw understanding beginning to creep across his face. He saw something flit across her expression as well before she put on her professional face again. What was it? Hope? Sadness? Pity? Despair?

Her well-trained hands found his arm and checked his pulse.

"Come on, now," she said, "you know the routine." She hummed, grunted, and felt for the glands near his chin. "How are you feeling?"

"Fine," he said.

"Same as usual?" she translated.

"Don't miss a twick, do you?" he asked, hoping

his Elmer Fudd delivery slipped by her ears. He had wanted to say "trick." That much was firmly in his head. But it had come from his mouth as "twick." He hoped she hadn't noticed. Or, if she had, that she thought it was a natural mistake.

"No," she said, "not a twick." So much for hope.

She sighed. "That's what I wanted to talk to you about." She returned to the seat opposite him and opened the manila folder she had laid on the table. "We have done enough studies to hazard a diagnosis."

Hazard? Studies? These were not words used by a jaded doctor. Not in a hospital library late at night. Doctors usually passed on information only under pressure, and then they came on like demigods. No hazarded diagnoses from studies. Rather, facts derived from tests.

"Be gentle, Doc," Archer said. "This is my first time."

She laughed, a trifle uneasily. "Now that's the man I've known these past few months," she said.

Yup, good ol' Archer. Always good for a chuckle as they performed test after study after analysis. "Am I really?"

"I'm afraid so," she said. "Tell me, has anyone in your family ever had a condition called chorea?"

Archer really thought he had misunderstood the question. His mind had been like that the past fortnight. "Anyone in my family been to Korea?"

"No, chorea. C.H.O.R.E.A. It's a medical condition, not a country. Have any of your relatives ever had it?"

Now she was stepping on shaky ground. Archer

had been adamant about not discussing his background. He saw no reason to. It didn't relate at all to his present situation. But now, all of a sudden, questions concerning his heritage came into play.

She saw his reluctance. "I wouldn't ask," she assured him, "unless it was important."

"Impoortant?" The word dribbled out of his mouth. He said it as Bruce Lee would have. The *r* sound almost didn't arrive at all. The *o*'s stretched out. He shook his head. "Why?"

The doctor sighed again. "We think you have a hereditary disease," she said. "If any of your relatives had it, then we would be certain."

Archer shook his head. "What is it?"

"Hunter's chorea," she said.

Archer's laugh was a bark. An involuntary burst of sarcastic mirth. Hunter's chorea! That was perfect, absolutely perfect!

"Are you all right?" she asked hesitantly. "What's funny?"

"It's nothing," he replied quickly. "Just a funny name for a disease, that's all. Sounds like something that tracks you down."

"Yes, it does, I suppose. I never thought of it that way." No, she only knew it as a condition, not a hunter. "In a way, it does. Track you down, I mean. Through your family."

His family? What family? Nothing tracked Archer through his family anymore. Parents? Dead. How? He wasn't sure. His grandmother raised him in California. Gave him money to attend karate classes. Sent him to Columbia University. He stayed in New York City. Trained at an Eighty-sixth Street dojo. Became assistant to the master there.

Archer had been lucky. His master had concentrated on the philosophy of martial arts as well as the subject of self-defense. He was teaching an outlook, not a way of breaking bricks and bone. He had no patience for any student who wished to do harm . . . of any sort. Those who wanted to protect themselves and attain a higher level of spiritual awareness were his favorite pupils.

Jeff Archer had been his best student. So good, in fact, that he became a partner in the studio after only four years. Soon he was able to command so many students' respect that he opened his own school on Twenty-third Street, allowing his master to retire or take on only the most gifted graduates of Archer's course.

In just six years, Archer had gained the self-assurance that had been eluding him for his formative years. He was finally secure enough to seek connections with his past. He decided he was going to ask his grandmother how his parents had died.

Before he could make the call, his grandmother had been raped by a street gang in San Francisco. His seventy-eight-year-old grandmother. And when she threatened to be a witness against them in court, the gang poured gasoline over her and burned her to death. Archer had returned home, seeking vengeance. He wasn't good enough.

The street gang, that bunch of sociopaths locked

together to attempt greater and greater atrocities—
the kind of people who would be so hateful that
they'd sexually assault an elderly woman—were
far more savage than he. He had right on his side,
but they had the eye of the tiger. Not to mention
chains, lead pipes, ax handles, baseball bats, and
knives.

It is said that a psychopath alone in a room filled
with rational beings is helpless. He is too afraid to
do anything, to be marked as a psycho. But put a
crazy in a room with other crazies, and there's no
telling the horrors that will be unleashed. When a
psycho discovers that he is "not the only one," it is
the beginning of the end.

So it was with this street gang. Fate brought
together the worst scum the slums held, and
together they moved from terrorizing one neighborhood to an entire section of the city. The mobs
knew a good thing when they saw it. Soon, the
gang handled numbers, drugs, hookers, and most
of the other ills the mean streets were known for.
Step out of line, and wind up headfirst in a
drainpipe.

Even the cops were leery of them. These guys
were nuts, you understand. The badges and blue
uniforms were no protection. They'd as soon go
after your wife, your children, your mama—even
your grandmama—if you got under their skin.

They got Archer's grandma. He got under their
skin. The only thing that kept him from being real
dead was his martial arts training. In that hospital,
so long ago, the first person to visit him was one

Brett Wallace. This had not been the same man he had saved from the gold needle eight months ago above the Rhea Dawn. This Brett Wallace had been a gregarious, fun-loving man-about-town.

This Brett Wallace had been a man to whom the Playboy Philosophy was a Bible. He wore the best clothes, he drove the best cars, he made love to the best women, he dined at the best restaurants, he was only seen at the best places. It was this Brett Wallace who donned a black outfit and helped kill the street gang. It was this assured, supremely accomplished Brett Wallace who grinned at Jeff when the last punk went down with a throwing star—a *shuriken*—in his forehead.

That Brett Wallace had been taken back to Japan for retraining... before the Dawn Dojo was signed over to Archer alone, before the Ninja Master began to sink in a mountain of criminal perversion, before he stepped up from street gangs to the mob to mass murderers to the worst monsters America had to offer, before the horror began to infest the *jonin* like a virus, before it all ended in a broiling mass of flame—and disease.

"What is it?" Archer asked.

The doctor swallowed her questions. "It's... it's a degenerative nerve disease," she said, then paused. Archer just stared at her, half his face in shadow. "It's a specific syndromatic disease; a chronic, progressive chorea."

Archer leaned in, his face in the lamplight. He was grinning. He couldn't help himself. It was funny. "Is that supposed to mean something? Did you suddenly switch to pig Latin? I can read your face fine. That says it's bad. But what the fuck is it?"

The doctor's brows met above her nose, and her lips tightened. She seemed to want to speak, but her training was holding her back. Archer saw the clouds clear just before she looked above his head in surprise.

"That's quite enough, Dr. Phillips," said a voice behind Archer's back. Archer looked over his shoulder to see a middle-aged man with black hair; a jowly, somewhat friendly face with an expression professionally fixed somewhere between sympathy and glaciation. The name tag on his white coat read "Dr. Bernstein."

By the way he acted, spoke, and practically lorded over the table, he was the head honcho, the big cheese. And he was very displeased with the way the woman had presented herself.

"Could you turn on the lights, please, Anthony?" he requested of the man behind him. Bernstein did not turn. He only had eyes for Phillips. It was Archer who looked at the man flicking on the overheads. He was short, balding, and paunchy. He was not a doctor, by the looks of him.

No white coat here. His polyester-blend three-piece-suit was a strange shade of brown and hung on him as if he had lost some weight recently. The lights went on with a push of his palm against the bank of switches. In his other hand was a clipboard.

Archer closed his eyes against the flash, waiting

for the glow behind his eyelids to subside. He heard Bernstein's sonorous attack upon his physician.

"Now, Doctor, I am fully aware that informing the patient of his condition is important, but at this time . . . in this place . . ." His tone was one of severe disapproval.

"I'm sorry, Dr. Bernstein," said Anthony, not Phillips, as he approached. "That may have been my fault. I asked the doctor to speak with him before I had to."

"Please, Inspector, we have our regulations," Bernstein told him without taking his eyes from Phillips. She seemed to be shrinking under his powerful gaze. "To discuss his condition without consulting me is one thing, but to tell him here, in this way, well . . ."

"Really, Doctor," Anthony pressed, "I must admit I didn't give her much choice. She probably didn't have time to confer with you."

Archer opened his eyes. He stared at the books before him. He was beginning to like this Anthony guy, this Inspector Anthony.

"Please, Inspector!" Bernstein snapped. "I don't tell you how to run your department, *don't* tell me how to run my hospital!"

One thing could be said for Inspector Anthony. He may have been short, he may have been paunchy, he may have been balding, but he knew how to get his back up. "Look, Dr. Bernstein, I'm *not* telling you how to run this place. I am *trying* to inform you of—"

"It must have been a very hard day, Doctor,"

Archer interrupted without turning around. It was a little trick...no, more a method involving *ki* taught to him by the Ninja Master. It was a method that required an extraordinary amount of control to counter. Control that Bernstein didn't possess at the moment.

"Well," he said, "it *has* been a long one...."

"Please don't punish Dr. Phillips and Inspector Anthony for doing what they thought best." Archer glanced up to see Phillips watching him with barely concealed gratitude. Her eyes had been tied to Bernstein's as if lashed by cord. Archer had sliced the connection as surely as if he had used a *katana*. She looked ready to slide out of her chair with relief.

He did not see Anthony's expression. While the young man looked at the woman and the woman looked at the hospital boss, the cop looked at the back of Archer's head. There was something about this duck that was familiar. Something...

"Well," Bernstein huffed, "I expect we've all had a pretty rough time of it today, eh, Inspector?" He did not wait for a reply. Instead he looked back at the woman, who snapped to seated attention. "Perhaps it would be best if you explain the situation to me over coffee in my office. Is that amenable with you, Doctor?"

"Yes, sir," Phillips answered, her voice strong. By Bernstein's new manner, it seemed to her that she would have no problem pinning the whole thing on Anthony. Anthony had warned that Archer had a lot of explaining to do, and he didn't want the man leaning on the crutch of his own condition.

Phillips had countered that it was unfair to confront Archer without his first knowing the state of his own health. Anthony had made it perfectly clear that he and Archer were going to have a chat that very night, whether he was up to it or not. Only then did Phillips decide to check Archer's condition and bring him up to date.

"Is that all right with you, Inspector?" Bernstein inquired amiably.

"That's what I was looking for all along," the man replied.

"Very good then," Bernstein concluded, turning toward the library door. Phillips took a final look at Archer, her expression saying that their business was unfinished and she was anxious to conclude it on her own terms.

Archer grinned reassuringly as she rose, his lips threatening to lock and then quiver in that position. He forced them to return to a guileless pose as the two doctors left. Anthony took over her chair on the other side of the table. He seemed intent on his clipboard. Finally he tossed it down; it made a sharp slapping noise when it landed.

"Something I can do for you?" Archer said slowly, as if he were a bored bank teller.

"May be," Anthony said, just as soberly. "I'm Inspector Anthony of the San Francisco homicide division."

"Anthony," Archer mused, playing with the book's page edges. "Surname or given?"

"You first," the cop suggested.

Archer ignored the suggestion. As if supremely indifferent, he rose languidly from his seat.

"They tell me you've been giving them some trouble about your name," Anthony continued. "They say you won't reveal your first or last name and that you will only respond to the word..." The cop checked his clipboard notes. "*Yasuru.*"

Archer walked away, moving toward the drawn and shaded windows. Anthony shook his head. Why did they have to be so difficult. He decided to continue his friendly approach before hauling out the big guns.

"What is that? *Yasuru?*"

Archer shrugged by the window. "It's what they call me."

"Come on," Anthony urged. "What does it mean?"

Archer shrugged again. "What does 'Anthony' mean?"

The cop clapped his hand hard on the tabletop. "Anthony means business!" he barked, rising. He stalked toward the young man, reading from the clipboard as he came.

"Your name is Jeff Archer. You have no relatives or next of kin. Until recently you were the owner and sole teacher at a kungfu studio called the Dawn Dojo. Then, all of a sudden, your place burns down. The department says it looks like arson. All right, fine. Places like yours burn down all the time. But less than two weeks later, a Japanese restaurant called the Rhea Dawn also burns down. The only one left in the debris is one

Jeff Archer. One Jeff Archer who wakes up in the hospital two weeks later demanding to be called 'Yasuru.' "

Jeff had retreated to the table. When Anthony approached him again, he moved toward the opposite end of the room. He stood in front of the television set there, the one chained to the bolted-down table.

"What do you say, Yasuru?" Anthony mocked, lowering the clipboard atop the books.

"What do you say, Anthony?" Archer replied. He rationalized that he was trying to see how much the cop knew. Quite a lot, as it turned out.

The cop accepted the challenge. "All right, Yasuru. I say you're the only common denominator between the two fires. I say you know more about them than you're telling. I say that it is not as simple as that. You were there, but the owner and chef were not. The owner and chef were never found. I say you know about one Rhea Tagashi and one Shiban Kan Hama."

Archer's laugh was a bark. So that was Hama's first name. Anthony could have saved himself a lot of trouble if he had only bothered to check a Japanese dictionary before he arrived. Then he would have known that *yasuru* meant archer, the arrow shooter. He would have also known that Shiban Kan, or *shiban-kan*, as it was more commonly known, meant judge. Judge Hama was passing sentence on the Ninja Master and his student.

"What's so funny?" the cop asked distrustfully. "I don't think you have much reason to laugh."

"Strangely enough," Archer replied, "neither do I. That's why I am."

Archer turned on the television set. The eleven o'clock news was in full flower.

As he stared blankly at it, Anthony suddenly knew who the young man reminded him of. That man in Sausalito, the one with the comatose girl friend. What was her name? Wendy? . . . No, McDonald. Not Ronald, but Lynn McDonald. She had been a beautiful girl. She still was, he supposed, if your interests ran toward eighty-pound vegetables.

Anthony glanced at his clipboard. Beneath it was the Merrick book. His eyes caught only a few words during his glance. "To the ninja, secrecy was their most valued commodity. They protected it with an obsession that bordered on the psychotic."

That's right, Anthony suddenly remembered. This duck was similar to that guy in Sausalito, just not as scary. That guy had been *very* scary. Anthony remembered how unnerving it was to look into this man's past and to find absolutely nothing. Not almost nothing, not virtually nothing, but *absolutely* nothing—zero, nada, rien, zilch.

But what he really remembered was facing the man over the hospital bed, across the girl in the coma. Anthony remembered the man's question. "What do you want to know?" He remembered his answer verbatim. "Nothing. Absolutely nothing."

What he remembered even more clearly was the emotion, the feeling. He remembered the icicle bobsledding down his spine and then slaloming across his legs. He remembered the cords in his neck bunching like rubber bands wound too tight. He remembered the fear that gripped his insides like hands.

No, this guy wasn't so scary. He was just a hard-nosed punk like all the others. A punk at the end of the line.

"Look," Anthony declared, "I know you're involved. I know you know more than you're saying. And I know I won't let go of this thing until I get the truth."

"What truth?" Archer finally addressed him directly, coming back from across the room. "Sure, perfect. I burn down my own dojo, which was doing very well. Then I burn down the restaurant, bury two corpses, and then drop the ceiling on myself."

"Who said anything about corpses?" Anthony asked innocently. He had him now. The guy had tripped up on his own words as so many had before. At least, on television.

"You're from homicide," Archer said with amazement.

That's right. He had said that when he introduced himself, hadn't he? What a dufuss. If he had been Columbo, he could have made his stupidity look like brilliance. But life wasn't a *Columbo* episode. He looked to the TV for help.

"These people" said a blond female television reporter striding before a lineup of uncomfortable-looking folk, "these brave people, are just like you and me—housewives, bankers, teachers—except for one thing. They are willing to place their lives on the line for what they believe is right."

Cut to a close-up of a woman's nervous face; dirty blond hair, bright blue eyes; a long nose. She laughs uncomfortably. "It's just that... when we see what is going on down there, well, you know, if there's a soldier and... and a little girl or her mother, we'll just put ourselves between them. That's all."

Cut to another close-up. A man's face this time; glasses, beard, earnest expression. "How can you... how can anyone see what is going on down there without... without wanting to do something?"

Cut back to the reporter, standing earnestly in the rectory of a small church. Behind her a group is packing, studiously avoiding the camera. "These people, this small group of parishioners from Saint Joseph's Congregational in Tatawan, Long Island, *are* doing something. To their friends and associates, they are known as 'Peacemongers.' Unlike the men (she hit the word *men* with notable force) who prolong or prosper by the conflict in Central America, these United States citizens hope to make a difference simply by being there."

Cut to a man labeled at the bottom of the screen as the first woman's husband. The woman reporter asked, "Are you happy that your wife is going?"

Anthony had to scoff out loud at that one. What assholes these reporters were.

The man replied, "Of course not! But she believes in what she's doing, and I'll back her one hundred percent on that!"

"Do *you* believe in what she's doing?"

"Well . . . that's not so easy . . . I don't know, really . . . I just don't know."

Cut to a priest with an egg-shaped head; black, greasy hair; a wide smile; and cleft chin. His jacket was off. "This is just one group from our congregation of churches. We cannot say what is right or what is wrong. That is up to the Lord to decide. But we must attempt to do his good works when the opportunity presents itself. We must seek to aid and comfort our brothers and sisters with the Lord's good words whenever and wherever we can."

Cut back to the reporter. She stands outside the church, on its little lawn. "So the Peacemongers go where military advisers fear to tread. To El Salvador—hoping, praying that wherever the guerrillas and death squads may be, they can make a difference. Not by attacking, but by putting themselves between the El Salvadoran citizens and possible atrocity."

Cut back to a replay of the first woman's words. "We'll just put ourselves between them. That's all."

Cut back to the reporter "'We'll just put ourselves between them. That's all.' Let's hope that it will be enough. Katie Baker, KTN News."

Cut to white-shirted anchorman. "Thank you, Katie. In other news . . . ."

Anthony looked over at Archer, who was staring at the television set as if mesmerized. *The power of the tube,* the cop figured. Time to bring the boy back from the dead zone.

"I hear the Rhea Dawn Restaurant wasn't doing so well."

Archer blinked, then looked over. "It was closed. That doesn't mean it wasn't doing well."

"Well," Anthony said reasonably, "when a place closes, you have to figure it wasn't doing well."

"It was doing *very* well," Archer countered. "There's more than one reason for a place closing. Say . . . a death in the family."

Anthony frowned. "Let's just say it wasn't doing very well. Let's just say that. And let's just say you find a nice way of collecting your insurance money. Arson or no arson, you collected. That's why this hospital doesn't care what name is on your Blue Cross card or where it is. They're getting paid.

"Now let's say things are going so well for you that you decide to go into the arson business; and this Rhea and this Shiban decide to hire you to torch their place. And let's just say things don't go quite the way you planned."

"I'm tired," Archer said suddenly. "I don't have to talk to you."

"Yes, you do," Anthony disagreed. "Sooner or later, here or downtown, you'll have to talk. If it wasn't for your doctor-plaything, I'd have you in the station's bowels tonight!"

"I've heard enough," Archer said miserably. "Leave me alone."

"You haven't heard enough!" Anthony countered, his voice rising. "You haven't heard nearly enough!

Oh, I may go now, but you haven't heard the last of me. Oh no! That's why my partner will be parked right outside your door all night. Just in case you start thinking about checking out."

Archer turned to face him, his right arm shaking violently. The cop misread it as the young man's attempt to keep from lashing out at him.

Anthony rose majestically from his seat, Lieutenant Anthony of the San Francisco homicide department, promoted and transferred after he mopped up the "slasher-movie murders" that stretched from Sausalito to Santa Cruz three years ago.

"Go ahead," he said tightly. "Make my day."

Great lines don't die. They simply cliché away.

Anthony kept staring until the arm's shaking went way beyond propriety. "Go ahead," he finally said. "Hit the sack. But be ready to talk first thing in the morning. I'm not through with you yet. Not by a long shot. I *know* you've got a story to tell. And this won't be over until you tell it."

Lieutenant Anthony collected his clipboard and left the room. Only then did Archer sit heavily and grab for his quaking arm. In two minutes, it subsided. Archer stared at the television set, feeling truly lost for the first time since he returned to the West Coast. His grandmother, his only link to his own past, had died. But he had acquired a new family and a new heritage. Where were they now?

Archer closed the books and went to his private room. The hospital hallways were dark. Bernstein and Phillips were long gone. But Sergeant Devlin of the San Francisco police was waiting outside his door. He opened the portal for Archer with a sarcastic smile.

The door clicked shut behind him quietly, but to Archer it sounded like a jail cell slamming. He was in his hell now, the sanitarium room where his own body betrayed him, where the hooded headsman had his face and the ax was something inside his own skin. He walked to his bed and checked his own chart. Words. Just words he couldn't possibly understand.

Bilateral atrophy. Concave caudate nucleus. Shrunken putamen. Mendelian dominant. Hepatolenticular degeneration. Choreoathetosis. Hemiballismus.

What sword could cut these? What *shuriken*? Where was the Ninja Master now?

The man was gone, but the hard-learned lessons were still there. The room was dark, lit only by the moonlight that came from the one window to the right of the bed. To its right was the bathroom door. To his left was the closet door. To his immediate left was a small writing desk and chair.

All right. Only three places a person could hide. Archer went to the closet and opened it. The only thing inside was a plastic hanger. He could take off his hospital-issue robe and hang it up. Hell, he could take off his hospital-issue pajamas and paper slippers and dance naked in the night if he wanted to.

Instead he went to the bathroom and urinated. One did not piss or pee in a hospital. One urinated.

When finished, Archer walked back to the bed.

He threw back the bedcovers. He stared at the
white, pristine, inviting surface of the soft bed. He
almost lay down, but the hard-learned lessons
were not so easily shrugged off. Grinning at his
own foolishness, Archer leaned over and checked
under the bed.

A figure in black with a *ninja-to* swung at his
face.

7

Archer could have made a lot of noise. He could have flipped back while shouting and screaming and making a big fuss so Sergeant Devlin could have come barreling in with his big revolver waving in his hand.

Maybe Archer could have kept the figure in black occupied long enough for Devlin to see him or, better yet, to shoot him. Then again, the figure in black might kill both Devlin and him. But at least then he'd no longer have to worry...about anything.

However, maybe the figure would kill only Devlin, leaving Archer to explain when Inspector Anthony got there.

At any rate, Archer didn't consider raising an alarm. He was trained as a ninja. A ninja did not raise a stink. A ninja never threatened the security of his *ryu*, disbanded or not. A ninja fought somewhere between heaven and hell, somewhere outside purgatory. It wasn't much, but it was all a ninja had.

So instead of crying out, Archer simply back-flipped.

He was lucky. The figure had been waiting for him to lie down, so the *ninja-to* had been embedded in the mattress, ready to thrust up through the bed to lance Archer's prone form. If it had not been thus, the figure would have rammed the blade through Archer's head or at least cut off his balls as the *genin* flipped back.

Archer sprang across his shoulders and catapulted himself to his feet. The bathrobe came off his back like a cape and swirled forward as the figure slithered out from beneath the bed and rose. His arm chopped the air. The sword in his hand sliced through the netlike robe, cutting it in half. It fell to the floor on either side of the standing figure.

Archer grinned with honest intent. The chorea did not control his lips this time. He viewed his opponent with honest pleasure. Now he knew. He wasn't dying quickly enough for them. He wasn't cut off from the insidious action. They still had to kill him themselves.

The sword was down. It must slice to the side or come up. Archer's stance was low and solid. He shot his fist forward. The sword swirled around it, waiting for the move. It was ready to go in any direction it might be needed.

Archer continued the arm-thrust. The sword snapped toward it. Archer's right leg kicked out and up. The sword danced between the fist and foot. The fist chopped at the blade, the foot suddenly lightninged in another direction.

The heel slammed into the swordsman's knee. The knee locked back. The figure slid backward, hitting the end of the bed. He rolled over it backward, landing upright on the other side.

It made no difference. Score point one for Archer. Archer didn't score in place. He leapt forward, sailing over the bed, his arms and legs tucked as high as possible. He couldn't expose their length to the sword. The stunned attacker slashed at the flying figure, not daring to pivot on the wounded knee since it might collapse beneath him.

Archer's right leg shot out and then immediately back. The sword swung at the now out-of-reach target. The left leg snapped forward and back. The sword just missed it as it left the figure's stomach. The swordsman staggered back, feeling as if a baseball had been hit into his solar plexus.

Archer landed on his feet and kicked to the side. Then stepped, then kicked, then stepped and kicked again. He drove the figure back toward the room's front door. He did it all without screeching, without shrieking, without even grunting. The pent-up rage of the last eight months exploded from him in silent little atomic bunches. He had been planning for this day since he had awakened in the hospital.

The swordsman had to hold his ground if he

didn't want to bump into the door and alert Devlin. But it was he who had the razor-sharp sword, the blade so keen it could cut through Archer's limbs with ease—if it could connect with them.

The sword did a special little defensive dance in the dark room, lit only by moonlight. It kept the flashing feet of the angry young man from reaching the figure.

Archer suddenly stopped pressing with his kicks. He stood calmly, just out of sword range. He wasn't in any martial arts stance. He was just standing there casually, smiling.

Then he did the incredible, the unexpected, the amazing. He turned his back on his adversary. He walked toward the bed.

His antagonist froze in place, not daring to rush forward to cut Archer down. What the *genin* was doing was suicide. He hadn't fought like that simply to turn his back to die. He must have been suckering the swordsman in for some reason.

In fact, he wasn't, but he had been hoping the figure would think it so. It gave him enough time to get to the bed and calm his shaking fist. The fist would not unclench. It vibrated as if powered by batteries. Archer calmed himself. The quaking subsided. He turned back to his attacker, still smiling.

It was more than the swordsman could bear. He charged forward, the *ninja-to* acting like a cobra about to strike. It whipped through the air, cutting, swirling, chopping so that no man could gauge its true path. It seemed destined for Archer's trunk, but then swept toward the *genin*'s neck.

The *genin* did not offer his neck to the headsman. Archer started tall, but slid into a monkey move, a Tai Chi maneuver. He crouched first, then his hand moved forward. It seemed as if the hand were painfully slow. The swordsman could just see it creeping toward his chest.

Ah, but then it disappeared. He saw nothing. Instead, he felt the fingers nearly crushing his sternum into his heart as the sword harmlessly whisked over Archer's head.

The figure bravely retaliated, not letting the pain in his chest slow him. The sword ducked and whirred, forcing Archer to dodge and dance back. He arrived at his own bedside, his grin still firmly in place. The "slow ball" of kungfu, Tai Chi Chuan, had done its work.

"I've had months to practice," Archer said quietly.

The figure darted forward, his sword doing a virtuoso performance. It sought out Archer's heart like a heat-seeking missile. When he ducked, it followed. When he leaped, it followed.

Archer had to stay next or close to the furniture. If the sword connected with its metal, it would make a sound Devlin was sure to hear. It was all that saved him in the following seconds.

Then it seemed as if he tired. It seemed as if he sought to end the torturous conflict one way or another. It seemed as if he wanted the outcome quickly. He dodged within the swordsman's arm's reach. The swordsman had the blade out. He swung it back for a beheading blow.

Archer dropped, his right arm snapping down and then swinging up in a wide arc. The sword went just over his head, cutting an eighth inch of his brown hair. He somersaulted backward again, winding up between his bed and the window.

The figure in black moved back. He flexed his arms. A foot-long vertical slit in his black shirt opened, revealing a hairless yellow chest. A two-inch slit opened on his face mask, revealing a chin and grimacing lips.

The lips worked for a moment more, then smiled.

The *genin* made the scalpel rise magically between his fingers. Its smooth, sharp point gleamed in the moonlight.

It had been child's play to secure a scalpel in a hospital. Keeping it on his forearm with Band-Aids and rubber bands was not so easy. Nor was training so he could shoot it into his hand in a split second. But the Ninja Master had given him the muscle control. It was simply a matter of time, which he had plenty of. Or at least he used to. The time had now run out.

"So you have finally come, Yamabushi," Archer said with disgust. "Where is the cunt?"

She entered not thirty seconds later wearing a nurse's uniform. She carried a tray with pills, a urine bottle, a syringe, and a small vase with a single flower.

"Bitch," said Archer, "where is your death

sentence? In the needle? In the medicine? Or do you pack a twenty-five automag in your garter?"

"Yasuru," Rhea hissed, her eyes wide, "I did not want it this way."

"Fool," Archer lashed back, so quietly the words hardly reached her. "What good do your wants do if you do not act on them?"

"Eight months in the hospital, and now it is you who mouth Confucius," Hama said with distaste. "Do not trade your pathetic psychology with us. You cannot understand a thousand years of history."

"Fuck you. You'll hide behind that bullshit forever."

"It is not . . . !" the woman flared, then controlled herself. "We did not cause this. Brett caused this. We are only trying to make things right."

"Keep your rationalization to yourself, Judas," Archer said lightly.

"Yasuru!" Hama spat, almost coming forward. "Do not mock!"

"What are you going to do about it, asshole?" Archer let that sink in for a second. As long as he held the scalpel and held firm, he had them. "You mark Brett a dead man, you come to ceremoniously execute me, and for what? Orders. You're only following orders. Sounds familiar. Orders of who? Orders why? Don't you question? Don't you *think*?"

"We think," Rhea said defensively.

"We do not question," Hama said with titanium-hard assurance.

"Yasuru," Rhea pleaded, "try to understand. The ninja are greater than all of us. They know more, they see more than we could possibly know or see. They fight for the world, our world. Brett had fought with them; now he fights against them. He must be stopped!"

"And because I am his student, I am also a threat."

Rhea could not answer. Hama could. "Yes. You have proven it tonight. A ninja would gladly die for his *ryu*. It is a ninja's highest honor."

"Honor. Ninja," Archer said with disgust. "Those words can't be used together." Rhea gasped. Hama's face went white. It took all their willpower to keep from charging the man. He was ready. They stood across from one another in the darkened room, speaking so only their six ears could hear.

"Think about this, *bakas*." He had used the Japanese for "fools." "Samurai would die for their clans. Ninjas died when caught . . . or when they revealed the *ryu*'s secrets. The secrets were revealed to Brett, to someone outside the family, so *ninjutsu* would grow and prosper. But now they feel their trust was a mistake. They are frightened of him, the Ninja Master. They will kill him and all who know the ninja secrets.

"You . . . you are only *inus* and *dogus*. You are the ninja's ninja. You take out the garbage that is too disgusting for even them to touch."

It was too much for Hama to bear. He had been called a fool, then a dog and a tool. He would not endure such shame from a doomed man—a white-skinned round-eye with no heritage, no home, and no honor. He moved forward, his sword raised for the kill.

Archer dove, sliding under the bed. Hama hacked at him. Rhea charged for the other side. Archer rocketed out the bed bottom. He vaulted to his feet, slicing open the nursing uniform from the back.

Rhea spun with the syringe in one hand and the vase in the other. The liquid swirled toward the *genin*. He had to avoid it at all costs. He jumped right at Hama. The *ninja-to* arced toward his head, promising to slice it open just under his nose.

Archer grabbed his bed's metal footboard along the top and side. He cartwheeled in the air. The liquid splashed onto the bedcovers and floor. Both sizzled and smoked. The sword sliced through the metal tubing of the baseboard as if it were cardboard.

Archer had lost his vaulting hold, but it was already too late. His cartwheel completed so that he was beside Hama. Hama couldn't bring his sword back in time. Archer slashed him across the nose and cheek with the scalpel.

The *genin* danced away as the warrior-monk bounced on the bed. Rhea vaulted over the Japanese's stunned form to jab at Archer with the syringe. Archer still held the baseboard remnant. He parried her thrusts with it. He suddenly kicked out with his leg. She parried with hers. Their legs lashed out repeatedly, each parry frustrating the other's attack. Finally they cut off their attacks, but Hama dove in with one of his own.

The sword sped at Archer's heart. He dove over it, somersaulted across Hama's back, and kicked

Rhea as he passed. She fell to one knee. Hama's sword sank into the wall. Archer landed on the bed.

His legs gave way beneath him.

The Hunter's chorea had found him wanting, and attacked.

He could no longer control his body. It wasn't just shaking this time, it was the wholesale earthquake of his entire being. His limbs were jerking spasmodically. His lips curled, and his face twisted of its own volition. It would have been hilarious if he could breathe. But even his lungs were lurching.

Jeff Archer slammed to the floor, his bladder emptying. The stench of his feces quickly filled the air. He lay on the tile floor of the hospital room, contorting uncontrollably.

Rhea and even Hama were shocked. The woman came around the bed and stared, the syringe still in her hand. When Hama saw him, he couldn't even bring himself to taunt the *genin* by calling him a *baka* and *inu*. The disease was too frightening and pitiful. They looked on this young man with infinite remorse and compassion.

That, more than anything, made Archer all the more enraged.

"I am sorry," Hama said, positioning himself over the spasmodically moving *genin*. "I truly am. But there is no other choice. You must give up your life for your *ryu*."

Rhea looked away as Hama prepared to chop off Jeff's head. Archer concentrated all his dwindling concentration on his own throat. His brain was screaming the words. All he had to do was make his throat and mouth form them.

His limited success took far more strength than his battle with the others had.

"Yaw woont kil ma," he said with agonizing slowness. As he spoke, his face muscles calmed. His expression took form like birds coming to roost. It was an assurance that was frightening to see.

"Why, *baka*?" Hama could not resist this time. "Why won't I kill you?"

"Be cause yoo wan Breat. Ah am dye ink anyway. You wan Brea...Brett."

Hama slowed his preparations, intrigued. "So?"

Archer grimaced. "So?" he mocked. "Ah kno ware he issss."

The *yamabushi* and the Judas looked at each other.

"Ah know where he is," Archer said slowly, the horrible spasm passing. "You follow me. Then wall see who is the *baka*, and who is the *shitai*."

8

A *shitai* stood in Dr. Phillips' room.

It looked like a *shitai*, but it did not think or act like one. A *shitai* was motionless, rotting. A living *shitai*, a zombie, fed mindlessly off the living. A *shitai* was Japanese for "corpse."

Archer—Yasuru—stood in Dr. Phillips' room. The bay window was open behind him; the filmy beige drapes flowed in the warm night wind. The air ruffled her bedclothes. It tickled her hair as it lay on the fluffy blue pillows.

The room was small but pleasant. The raised, wooden ornate bed took up most of the space. On it lay Phillips and a man. Her man, Archer supposed. He did not have the furtive, pinched, swarthy look of a pickup or the plastic handsomeness of a one-night stand.

He looked thin, sensitive, intelligent. A lot can be inferred from a sleeping face.

More could be inferred from the way they slept. She held him, her front to his back. Still more could be inferred from the room in which they slept. There was more than simply makeup and "women's things" in the room. Male clothes were hung in the closet, as well as dresses. Men's shoes and sneakers and slippers were also under the bed.

They were married or they lived together. The *genin* couldn't help being disappointed. He had braved the night for her. He was going to brave all after he left her. Was it not only right that the warrior should have something to live for before going into battle?

Getting into the apartment house had been easy. Not simple, but easy—easier, certainly, than escaping the hospital. After his confrontation with the traitoress and the *yamabushi*, he longed to feel Devlin's bones smashing beneath his fists. But he realized that was both impractical and sadistic. He was redirecting his anger at an innocent, an innocent who could raise an alarm conscious or unconscious.

If Devlin didn't report in or was found beaten, it would alert everyone. Instead, Archer exited after Hama—through the window. The Japanese was taking the risk. He was dressed in black, clearly discernible on the sandstone walls of the clinic. Archer was still in his beige pajamas, hardly blending with the night, but like a chameleon on the wall.

The two took a final look at each other as they reached the ground. Hama had his sliced face-covering off. His eyes said that Archer would not see him, but he would be there, waiting and watching, every step of the way. Hama did not then slip off or run off or slink off. He walked away calmly, seemingly oblivious to the sword on his back and the cut across his face.

Rhea had exited the way she had come, as a nurse. Archer had no doubt she would join Hama in a car. He also had no doubt that they would not be tailing him tonight. At least not personally. Archer smiled at the thought of the stoic Hama waiting until they returned to whatever "safe house" they were using before collapsing in tears, grabbing for his torn face in pain.

It probably wouldn't happen, but it gave Archer a certain satisfaction. Dropping the fantasies from his mind, the *genin* considered the problem at hand. He kept to the side streets and back alleys, just as the Ninja Master had trained him. After a few weeks of intensive research with his *shihan*, Archer knew the San Francisco streets better than any dozen cabdrivers.

Acquiring clothes was fairly rudimentary as well. The research included breaking and entering: finding an army-navy store in a depressed neighborhood—one not likely to spend thousands on an alarm system or even a Doberman; then either picking the lock, slithering through the air vents, or just breaking down the back door.

Archer stood in Phillips' apartment wearing all black: black long-sleeved T-shirt; black pants; a lightweight all-weather black jacket with zipper and buttons; and black walking boots.

In his jacket pockets were a kerchief, a compass, a Totes rain hat, work gloves, a wooden *kubotan* short-stick, and six *shuriken*. On his wrist was a military watch covered by a tactical watchband— the kind that covers the face so the crystal doesn't reflect light. In his boot was a survival knife with black handle and sheath. It's amazing what army-navy stores sell these days.

Oh yes, in his pants pockets was all the money from his secret "bank account." It was the kind of account that didn't need a withdrawal slip or three kinds of identification. He had opened it at the Ninja Master branch office four years ago and had been making deposits ever since. It was a treasure he had buried somewhere in Frisco for something like this very occasion.

How do I knock thee out? Let me count the ways. Archer laid two firm fingers on the artery supplying blood to the sleeping man's brain. He counted off silently. He released the man's neck when he was certain the fellow would sleep through anything up to and including an earthquake. Then he knelt by Phillips and whispered in her ear.

They were soothing, reassuring words. They told her who he was and what he wanted. Then he carefully placed his hand across her mouth and woke her up. The subconscious preparation served him well. When her eyes opened, she hardly panicked. She started and kicked a bit, but almost instantly she recognized him. His manner and expression told her more. There would be no attack, just talk.

He sat on the edge of the bed as she sat up, gathering the bedclothes at her chest. She looked over at her man before returning her astonished gaze to Archer.

"Are you out of your mind?" she whispered.

"No banter. No small talk," he said seriously, quietly. "I have to go." He cut off her questions with a quick explanation. "I did not burn my studio, I did not burn the restaurant, and I did not kill those two people. As a matter of fact, they just tried to kill me. I have to leave San Francisco now."

"What... what do you want from me?" He could see that she feared robbery as well as rape.

"Information."

"I... I don't know what—"

"I have to know what will happen to me. What will the chorea do to me? How long do I have? What can I do?"

Realization lit her face. "You must go back to the hospital!" she said, gripping his arms. "You can't—"

"I can't go back to the hospital and I can't risk breaking into a library to find out what Hunter's chorea is." The hard edge of *ki* came back to his quiet voice. "Tell me."

She wore a lovely nightshirt; blue with lace flowers; spaghetti straps across her shoulders, a wide U neckline. Her breasts were round, high, and firm. The tears that collected in the corners of her eyes, the emotion, made her skin glow and her manner soften. Archer ached all over.

"It's . . . it's a degenerative disease of the nervous system. But it doesn't have the liver disease or biochemical abnormalities others can have."

"What *does* it have?"

"You lose nerve cells. You start having involuntary movements. Your face will pinch up. There will be grimacing. You won't be able to form words clearly."

Archer nodded. That had started already.

"It will spread to your body. Your limbs will jerk. You will have no control of your arms and legs."

"Can I control it? Does it remain consistent?"

"No. No, it will get worse. But it is slow. And after a particularly violent incident, it will seem to improve and lessen."

Archer nodded. Like now. After his contortions on the hospital floor, he felt fine. Good as new. "What else? What else?"

"You will get headaches and fevers. Your breathing will become difficult. It will be hard for you to breathe. And as the muscular problems worsen, you . . . you will . . ." She started to cry.

He put a hand over her naked shoulder. Her skin was warm and smooth. He felt like crying too. "There's no nice easy way of saying it, is there?" he commiserated. "I'll lose my mind, won't I? One day I'll just start dropping pieces here and there, leaving a trail behind me."

She couldn't nod. She leaned forward and held him, crying. "I'm sorry," she finally said. "I'm sorry."

He carefully extricated himself from her wonderful embrace. "My name is Jeff Archer," he told her. "'Yasuru' means arrow shooter in Japanese."

"Archer," she repeated, blinking her tears away. "My name is Jane." She tried to smile, saying the next words bravely. "You Archer, me Jane."

He laughed. She laughed too, the smile cracking her sorrow. It would return soon enough. "I'm sorry, Jeff," she said.

Archer nodded and shrugged. "It was important to know." He got up from the bed.

"Wait a minute!" she suddenly remembered. "It can't stop it, but chlorpromazine can help control it. Fifty milligrams three times a day. That'll help." She hopped out of bed. Her mini-nightshirt swirled about her long legs as she went to the bureau on the other side of the room. "I can write you out a prescription!"

Archer laid a hand on hers. He shook his head.

"I can say you filled it before," she suggested weakly. "Predate it."

"I'll get it," he assured her. "Thank you." She nodded again. He left her standing there. He went to the bedroom door and stopped, looking at the apartment's front door. He looked back at her standing in the moonlight. She had completely accepted the magic of the moment. It was as if the man in her bed did not exist.

"I wish I knew how to make you forget," he said. "A Superman kiss."

"I don't want to forget," she said.

He started for the door, then stopped. Ah, what the hell. He went back across the room and left by the window. A romantic flourish, to be sure. But you only live once.

"Having wonderful time. Glad you're not here."

Archer had bought the postcard, addressed it and everything. The only thing he hadn't done was mail it. The address was the post office box the Ninja Master had rented. The addressees were "Bushy and Jude." That gave him a kick. Maybe it was actually humorous, and maybe he was losing his mind faster than Jane Phillips had anticipated.

Archer was amazed at how much his *shihan* had done before the attacks by the figure in black to prepare for such an eventuality as the Figure in Black. The "bank account," the post office box, and all the rest were ways the abandoned *genin* could stay alive and in touch with the *ryu* in emergencies. Only this postcard was a private joke Yasuru decided to save for himself.

On the back was the address and the message. On the front was a beautiful aerial view of lovely Puerto Angel, situated on the scenic western edge of the Tehuantepec Gulf. At least, that's what it said in the upper left corner of the card. From where Archer was standing, the place was pitifully similar to every other area of Mexico he'd been through.

Getting to the border hadn't been a huge problem. Archer headed east out of Frisco, went through Nevada, and took a sharp right at Utah. He kept going until he was almost past Arizona. He could have gone to Nogales, to Bisbee, to Douglas, even to El Paso, Texas. Or to any one of the dozens of border towns. But they would have had border guards.

Instead, he got off east of Yuma and walked across the border into Onora, Mexico. The patrols were used to Mexicans trying to get out. They were not so used to gringos coming in. Not this gringo, that's for sure. No one saw him, no one stopped him, no one did anything.

Archer walked and hitched rides under the hot southern sun until he could start picking up the rail lines into the heart, and then the lower intestines, of Me-hee-co.

What fun! What adventure! His black clothes soaked up the sun like solar panels. He bought a light, short-sleeve off-white shirt and pleated pants, as well as a small duffel to carry his stuff. Since he was so near the border, he was able to buy it with American dollars, bargaining the sidewalk salesman down to five bucks. Then he sought a quick, easy method of exchanging his U.S. currency for pesos.

The banker thought he was an idiot. That is, until he thought Archer was a psychotic killer. First he tried to gouge the young man with a ridiculous exchange policy. Then he recanted when he found his tie knot tightened halfway to his larynx. Archer got his Mexican money fair and square.

The banker sent some boys to talk to Archer at the room where he was staying, trying to show the lone Anglo the error of American policy toward their poor neighbor. In other words, the banker thought of the exchange as a loan. A poor college boy alone in a hostile environment with a pocket full of pesos had to be careful. That was the lesson. Only, that particular day Archer was doing the teaching.

They came into his hotel room in the pitch of night. Archer used the four knife-wielding bozos for karate practice. The first got a standing side kick to the head. He went back out the door. The second got what is known as a jump spinning crescent kick to the face. He dove into the water bowl on the bureau.

The third made the mistake of trying to slash Archer. He handled himself well, just like a veteran street fighter. He came in low with the switchblade. Archer caught his wrist in one hand anyway, then used his other fist to bring the boyo out of the room by repeatedly smashing him in the mouth.

He dropped the limp third man to follow the fourth, who was careering down the hall to the front stairs. Archer was right behind him as he reached the top step. Archer hopped in place. His left leg bent. His right leg lashed out, catching the man at the back of his neck. The fourth dove down the stairs like an Olympic swimmer.

His landing was a bit rougher, however. He caught the first floor landing's bannister uprights full in the face. He almost broke through, but then his body flopped painfully to the floor, his face pushed back to his ears.

Archer stood at the top of the stairs. "Room Service?" he called. "Can I have a maid, please?" He checked out before the police arrived.

What the thieves couldn't do, the water did. And if it wasn't the water, then it must have been the food or the atmosphere. Archer got to Durango before the auxiliary germs jumped him. He was barfing and defecating for four days, holed up in a nice hotel. The entire floor had to be practically disinfected before he left.

The only good thing about his holocaust version of The Revenge is that the chorea had the good taste to retreat while Montezuma beat him senseless. He took a plane to Mexico City. His pronunciation of English was bad enough without trying to force Spanish off his thick tongue. Sleeping on the flight kept him from starting or maintaining any conversations.

The bright modern architecture of Mexico City and its sister cities Toluca and Puebla cheered him somewhat. He lived comfortably for a few days, eating well, and thought of Jane Phillips.

When he saw the massive black locomotive the next morning, he thought of Inspector Anthony instead. He had cleaned his off-white outfit the night before. He folded his black outfit—along with his newly acquired camouflage-patterned shirt and slacks—into his duffel and carried it on his shoulder.

He ambled through the dusty open-air cars of the train. Most of the seats were filled, but it wasn't crowded. He was able to get a window seat and watch Mexico go by. His headache didn't faze him. Between the disease and the southern sun, his head had partnered up with a dull throbbing that danced whenever he expended effort.

None of the ninja training could make it go away, so he used more of the ninja training to live with it, to help it heighten his senses. He knew he had to try even harder to make his body work at optimum efficiency. By the time they crossed into Oaxaca, he could sense another bout coming on. Sudden jerkings and grimacing were great to keep the seat all to yourself, but sudden shitting often became embarrassing.

The railway cars were old, but not old enough to lack bathrooms. Unfortunately, they were old enough to have bathrooms that didn't work. The stench was incredible, but Archer could only be thankful that piles of excrement weren't dotting the enclosure like giant anthills.

The smell was nearly overpowering, and squadrons of flies dive-bombed the occupant every moment. Archer spazzed-out for eleven minutes in the sweatbox, slamming his limbs on the walls and floors, his mouth gibbering. Thankfully, the noise of the engine drowned out his pathetic babbling.

The shame and terror of the chorea attacks might have mentally crippled other men. They did manage to depress Archer. He had taken a moment to check a library in Mexico City. Hunter's chorea crawled on for years. If one could fend off the concurrent infections, one could die of old age ... although one would be too far gone by that time to be aware of it. Or anything else.

Mostly, chorea sufferers committed suicide before their brains slipped through their fingers. The horror was feeling it going, knowing it was going. The tip of that iceberg Archer could feel already. But he swigged down his chlorpromazine capsules and hoped.

Doctors could be very amenable when mucho dineros were waved in their faces. With his bankroll, he had been able to get a six-month supply of the tablets.

Thankfully, Archer had enough time to neaten himself and sightsee before the train made its last stop. The cities in Oaxaca had that baked charm so much of Southern Mexico had. Poverty-ridden charm, but a certain tragic charm nevertheless.

The train wound painfully through the mountains and past the farms. It was the Southern Sierra Madre—the Sierra Madre Del Sur—where gold once made men mad with greed.

The winds from the Pacific kept the temperature hovering around eighty all the time, and the cactus sands gave way to tropical palms as he made his way across the nation. The humidity built up like a growing giant, ready to swat the human ants between massive fat fingers.

No one sat near the young gringo madly chattering away in a Mexican accent about what a nice boy was doing way down here and why he didn't visit Acapulco instead. Archer saw to it that everyone wanted to stay clear. The disease's nervous ticks helped, but the ninja training did the true trick. By the time they wheezed into the last port of call, Archer was virtually alone in the car.

The Puerto Angel station was hardly what one would call impressive. The hot, motionless air filled his mouth and throat like an invading tube. The dust stung his already weathered tan face. The steps between sunburn and leather skin had been crossed some fifteen hundred miles north.

A tiny street market of sorts had grown up around the grain tracks and the beaten unloading platform. Around that were small tin and wood shacks backed by mangrove trees. Dark, Indian faces looked up at him as he stepped down, the platform boards creaking under his weight. Suddenly a mob of children were all around him, some offering goods but most begging.

He kept one hand firmly in his money pocket and kept the other gripping his duffel. He waded through the kids as if they were the Southern California surf.

"*Atras lejos!*" he kept repeating—back away. "No, no, no, no."

He managed to wade toward the little street's main store. It was bigger than the other dwellings, better built, and had a sign. It was only when he neared it that the children dispersed. A heavy, unshaven man with a thick mustache charged forward, batting them back with big, hairy arms.

"Senor," he said, his voice a low growl from too much vitamin D and humidity. "Come on in, uh? You must be tired."

On the other side of two screened doors was the town's main hangout. To the left under a balcony was the general store. Bags of goods lay on the floor at the base of shelves packed with necessities. On the far wall were farm tools as well as rifles.

On the balcony were doors—leading to rooms, no doubt. Probably guest rooms for visitors and working cells for prostitutes. It was too early in the day for any of them to be out working. They were still trying to sleep off last night's action, Archer supposed. In a town like this, it was all the men could do. Where was the football stadium? Where was the video arcade? Where was the jai alai fronton?

Before him were well-worn round tables and wooden chairs. To his right, along the entire wall, was a well-worn bar with stools. Behind the bar was a well-worn woman. Her expression and manner, however, told Archer that, well-worn though she may be, she was not beaten, not even mildly crushed. As soon as he appeared in the doorway, she set up a bottle of beer on the bartop. She smiled as Archer approached.

"Angel," the man said, following. "That's my wife. I tell her they named the city after her."

They laughed like people who had heard the same line a million times.

Archer took his first swig from the bottle. It was actually almost cold. When the sun beat down the way it did here, lukewarm could seem frosty.

"No, my friend. Actually," the man went on, "she is an angel of mercy instead. She is mother to the entire town, eh, my sweet?"

"Sister," she corrected him. "Sister to the entire town." Her voice was scratchy but warm. Archer smiled at her. She was a gem, all right. Her best years were behind her, but she had served the town well and they paid her back in loyalty and love. He could see it in her eyes and in her face. She was queen of Puerto Angel.

But *he* was not king. That much Archer could see about his host. He laughed at his wife's joke with the pleasure of a man who had made his prized pet jump through a hoop. Ta-da! Isn't that something, ladies and gentlemen?

"No, really, Senor. You call her Angel. And me, you call me Samuel. Like your Uncle Sam, okay?" He really laughed at that, clapping Archer on the back.

Archer looked at him and nodded. Although he had been terse in the years before he knew the Ninja Master, the disease had made him a regular Marcel Marceau. He didn't talk unless he absolutely had to. And he saw that necessity coming up any second now. When a stranger came to Puerto Angel, the bartender or shopkeeper would want to know why.

Instead, Sam bellowed, "Good! You sit, you

relax, you have your drink, eh? It's on the house, okay? It is our welcome to you. Then, if there is any way I can help you, you let me know, okay?" He moved away from the surprised Archer, back to the front door. "You entertain our guest, eh?" he said to his wife.

She nodded, and waved him outside. Archer looked at his exit and then back to the woman.

"He is loud, but with a heart of gold, you know?" she said. "He gives away beers. Big man, huh?"

Archer smiled a smile that said, "Don't worry, the tip will cover it." Again, he expected the interrogation: "So, what brings you to our quaint little village? Staying long? What's a nice boy like you doing in a place like this?"

But it did not come. Instead, a tiny voice spoke from the door. "Senorita?" Archer turned to see one of the children from the station standing halfway in the room.

"Aah, venis en," she said, automatically translating for the gringo. "Come in, come in."

The little boy's face lit up, and he came racing inside with a shoeshine kit. Adorable, Archer thought. He wore a dirty sleeveless T-shirt and dirty shorts. No shoes.

"Shine, senor?" The boy hardly waited for an answer. He knelt at Archer's feet, already pulling up his pant legs. He was faced with the big calf-high black boots. "Ay, carumba!" he breathed. Archer's footwear would use up most of his polish.

Archer smiled and shook his head. Before the boy could recover, the door opened again. Archer's smile faded. His Uncle Sam was back with the marines. The man's face said that he had done his duty, but now he was out of it, as usual. The faces of the two animals flanking the fourth man said they liked their meat raw and torn from the bone. And they liked a lot of it.

The man in front was shorter than the rest, shorter than Archer even. And he was wide. Not fat wide like the animal bookends, but muscle wide, solid wide. The men beside him were bearded. He had only a mustache. His chin was cleanshaven but flecked with heat rash. His chin said he shaved because he wanted to—it was his pleasure to tear his flesh so an image of decorum could be maintained.

That image was complete. He wore the crisp, clean, sweat-soaked uniform of the "Judicial Police of the Federal District and Territories." He had a black holster at his right hip with a gun firmly snuggled inside. He wore a shined brown wooden club at his left hip. Archer could just picture the animals taking turns cleaning it every day.

No wonder no one had inquired as to Archer's reason for being here. They were waiting for the lord of the manor. This, then, was the king of Puerto Angel.

Archer turned on the stool as the men on either side of the policeman sauntered forward. When the cop came, he marched. There was nothing easygoing or smug about him. Everything about him looked direct.

"Grande Hombre," the bartender said, "nice to

see you." The queen could talk back to the king, it seemed.

"Silencioso," he said. "I have business here."

It wasn't work he had here. He didn't say, "I have a right to be here." He never mentioned curiosity. He had business. Gringo equaled business.

But first the speech.

The big, fat men moved to within a foot of Archer. They used to be muscular, but now they were just big and fat. When they couldn't get what they wanted by intimidation alone, they must have fought by memory. They were eating well, and not just potatoes and beans. The policeman stood three feet away, behind his human guard dogs.

"Puerto Angel is a small, quiet town, señor. We are not like Acapulco and Cancun. We do not need tourists." He paused, keeping his face passive. "But we welcome you. We hope your stay will be pleasant. Will you stay long?"

"Depends," said Archer.

"On what?"

"If I find what I'm looking for."

The man noded. "Ah-huh," he said. He understood all. In that regard, he was one up on Archer. "You can get what you need if you have the money."

"You don't know what I need."

The cop looked away in distaste. This was getting less and less direct. He didn't like that. He didn't want to have to spell things out. Spelling things out was direct, but distasteful.

"I know what you want," he finally said angrily.

"You're a nice boy. Look at you. Nice Anglo college boy. You come down here with alligators on your shirt, polo players on your shirt, initials on your shirt and backside!" He slapped his rear. "You came to Puerto Angel because we have what you need. But first, first you have to give what we need, uh?"

The cop was irritated that he had to get angry. With a short nod, he unleashed the animals. He walked toward a table as the men grabbed handfuls of Archer's shirt.

Archer's initial move was stunning, but went all the way back to his first jujitsu lesson eleven years ago. The first animal's hand went across his chest. The *genin* grabbed the man's wrist with his nearest hand, and used the other fist to break the ape's arm at the elbow.

Suddenly the animal to his left was on the floor, on his knees. The move dragged the other man to *his* left. Archer's fist snapped back, his knuckles pushing the other animal's nose into his face.

The *genin* knew it wasn't going to be enough. These were the kind of dolts who could have railroad spikes in their brains without knowing it. The man began to step back, dragging Archer with him. Archer kept hitting him with the back of his fist so fast you could hardly see his arm move. He walked with him two steps, his fist sinking deeper and deeper into the man's face—BAM-BAM-BAM-BAM-BAM—until it finally got through to the ape.

It felt good after the hospital and the trip south to beat someone silly. A ninja was not supposed to

enjoy fights. A ninja was supposed to attain a
higher plane where violence for violence's sake
was not condoned. A ninja was supposed to do
whatever was necessary; no more, no less. But
fuck it. This was gratifying.

The ape let go. He stood there, his hands open
in front of him, wondering if anybody got the
name of that battering ram. Archer hopped into
the air and kicked the man's neck. He slammed to
the floor like a felled tree.

The first ape started getting up. Archer landed
lightly, then spun backward without completely
coming to rest. The jump spinning crescent kick
threw the first man across a table, headfirst into a
chair back and then into a series of somersaults
across the floor.

Archer landed on both feet firmly. Thump-thump.

Both the cop's and the woman's arms moved.
Click-click.

The cop sat pointing a .357 Magnum revolver at
Archer. The bartender was leveling a sawed-off
shotgun at the young man's back.

The *genin's* mind locked onto the weapons.
Snick-snick. The disease hadn't eroded his weapons
training yet. He held a Colt Mark III Lawman
with a four-inch barrel. Six rounds. She held a
Savage/Stevens Model 94C single-shot. Could've
picked that sucker up for sixty-bucks. All right for
a bar, though. It was noisy but would get the job
done. Either weapon would.

Archer slowly put up his hands. "Let's talk," he
suggested.

9

They followed the Beach Boys through the jungle.

I'm pickin' up good vibrations, she's giving me excitations . . .

Archer and the policeman walked alone. The apes were left behind to collect what tender mercies they could for their ruined faces and arms. The cop had treated Archer with deference as well as fear. They talked their business; the man collected his money; and they set off through the tropical woods.

All that time, the king saw no reason to give Archer his name. He saw even less reason after the young man's performance in the bar. Archer just thought of him by Angel-the-bartender's introduction: "Grande Hombre." Big man.

Hummmmm, bop, bop. Good vibrations, bop, bop.

The Beach Boys got louder as Grande pushed aside flora which then swung back into the gringo's face. Archer wished the Ninja Master had showed him some way to chop this pliant foliage aside without expending fighting *ki*. Oh, he could do it all right. Archer could hack the stuff apart as if his fingers were machetes, but it wouldn't be worth it. Instead, he blocked them with his hands and arms when he could, and with his face and neck when he couldn't.

Gotta keep those good things a'happenin' with her . . ."

They broke through the dense patch of vegetation just as the Beach Boys hit the choral climax of the song. Spread before Archer was a vision of loveliness: a sailing ship, the sloop *John B* moored at the edge of a Mexican jungle, lightly drifting on a blanket of sparkling blue water, blinding white in the burning southern sun.

Around her was a bunch of the gosh-darndest, gee-golly-whizzed, nicest clean-cut blond college boys Archer had seen this side of L.A. They toiled merrily in their short-sleeve rugby jerseys, their jersey-knit cotton Islanders, their six-pocket twill cargo shorts, their double-pleated Burma campaign shorts, and their brown eighty-dollar mocs.

The only person who didn't look prepped out was obviously the eldest there: a bearded man with a tan, lined face and gray hairs etched in his otherwise black mane. It was he the Grande Hombre spoke to.

"Hey, universidad muchacho!" he called over the blaring portable tape machine. The man, who was hauling a duffel bag up to the boat's deck, turned his head toward them. "I've got a friend of yours here."

The man squinted, then said a few words to the other boys. Archer counted four in number: all blonds, save for one with light brown hair; all young—about twenty years old at an average; all acting as if they were on spring break. The man's expression as he approached took on the character of midterm time. He was not happy.

He took the cop's hand and burbled a few Spanish words about how good it was to see him and how it was always an honor and how he wasn't worthy to lick guano off the cop's instep. Then he got down to cases. What was this about a *friend* of theirs . . . ?

"This fellow comes to town," the cop said, pulling a thumb from his gunbelt and pointing it at Archer. "He says he wants a ride to San Salvador. I figure he's with you."

"Well, you figured wrong," the man said.

"You mean . . . ?" the cop gasped, reaching for his gun.

One finger, that's all Archer used. He calmly placed his forefinger just above the cop's wrist as the Grande Hombre jerked for his pistol. He kept his eyes on the older American the entire time as the cop's fingers gripped the gun, pulled it from the holster, and then dropped it on the ground. Archer only glanced at the Mexican when it appeared he would try to retrieve the weapon.

That was enough. The Grande Hombre backed away from both Anglos.

"Who are you?" the bearded man asked, not frightened, not annoyed, just cautious. And maybe a bit territorial.

Archer saw it all clearly: the college lads; their mentor; the payoff to the cop; the quiet, cautious villagers. Puerto Angel was a perfect drug-running town. And a quartet of vacationing preppies with their university professor was the perfect cover. So they paid the Grande Hombre to use the minor, miserable port, and he didn't call the gringo-haters from the hills or the coast guard from offshore.

And just who *was* Archer anyway? The cop thought he was one of "them." The bearded Anglo knew he wasn't a member of *his* group, but he still thought he was one of "them." So why not be one of "them"? His youthful appearance fit the part and otherwise he'd have to do a lot of convincing.

"My name is Jeffries," Archer lied. "Like he said, I need a ride to San Salvador."

"There are a lot of planes and trains that go there. Why should we take you?"

"If you help me, I'll help you," Archer said. "People might be upset. I can handle them."

The bearded man looked at the cop. He nodded hastily. The man looked back at Archer. He was doing a good job of hiding his concern—a good job, but not a great one. It was obvious these five weren't "connected," weren't affiliated with the mob or with established drug traffickers. They were walking the black line between heavy profit and the deep six.

They didn't know who Archer was and they didn't want to know. They were more willing to do what he wanted and pray that he simply walked out of their lives in Central America than quibble over specifics. Just take the bottom line: he knew about their operation and he was real good with his hands. Better they should give him a lift than try to kill him or let him alert anyone.

"You're going to El Salvador," the cop said to the bearded man hastily. "Take him there." He made it an order. He ran a tight town and he didn't want trouble with anyone, least of all the mad-dog drug rebels in the hills or gringo mobsters. He let his boys grow fat on their earnings while he socked his away, waiting for the day he could retire to Sweetwater or Abilene and watch the big Texas women go by.

The bearded man, known as "the Prof," looked Archer over carefully. Dressed all in white, with a placid expression, he didn't look so bad. Certainly not cunning or evil. Looked at in the right way, the young man actually looked . . . friendly. The Beach Boys swung into "Wouldn't It Be Nice."

"Come on," said the Prof. "I'll introduce you around."

Astonishingly, the sloop *was* called the *John B* —named after both the Beach Boys song and

John Bendix, a wealthy industrialist whose philosophy formed the foundation of the crew's beliefs. This crew, unlike the corrupt sadists of the song, believed in fun, free enterprise, women, and beer —not necessarily in that order.

It was Bendix who gave the Prof the money for the motor sailer, and also gave him the inspiration for the boyos' quarterly money run.

"Go for it," he had said. "Go for all the gusto you can before you become an old fart like me." John Bendix would have been right at home in a beer commercial.

They had some four hundred miles of ocean to cross, and the crew handled the sailing without spilling a bit of wind. They traced the west coast of Mexico until they neared the border of Guatemala. They knew the way to San Jose, which nestled next to Iztapa near the El Salvador border. They did not resort to the inboard engines on the ship unless the sea was dead calm or deadly rough.

Squalls were held down to a minimum over the three-day trip, Mother Nature quelling the sea and the Prof keeping the crew in line. The Prof had introduced Archer around as an added crew member who would pull his weight without taking a cut of the profits, which was fine with the college quartet . . . at first. Once they had set sail, all began to wonder why Jeffries was being so magnanimous.

Archer soon allayed their concerns, and he didn't need much *ki* to do it. He felt great. The sea air, the sailing, and the sense of freedom were invigorating. He felt good, really good, for the first time since leaving the continental United States.

Hunter's chorea was almost a dream out here. He had to assume that the nerve disease was tied in with his "nerves," that is, feelings of tension and paranoia. Those emotions had to aggravate the degenerative aspect of the ailment. But out here... out here the nerve endings floated on a figurative and literal sea of calm.

Sailing was a new experience for Archer, but not one of which he was totally ignorant. The Ninja Master's training was at times superficial, but it was complete. Archer would not feel completely at ease in a plane, in a tractor trailer, aboard a locomotive or on a ship's bridge, but he wouldn't feel completely "at sea" either. He knew just enough about all modes of transportation to get by. And what he didn't know, the crew was willing to show him. It was less work for them, after all.

As it was, their sloop pretty much sailed herself. It was a beautiful, cunning design. There were sleeping berths below for three, leaving a crew of two to man the craft at all times as they slept in shifts. Midship between the forward and aft berths was the galley, consisting of a small stove, sink, icebox, and dining table—which doubled as a chart table—and the head. Topside, aft of the wheel and the throttle for the sloop's powerful inboard engine, were three access lids to the deceptive hold and, through them, to the bilge. The bundles could be dumped loose into the bilge—which was less likely to be searched but also less preferable due to the risk of bilge water contaminating the cargo—or stowed in secret compartments behind false panels in the hold.

These five weren't drug kingpins, but they liked to gather enough snort or smack to pay off big when divided among them. It wasn't a question of morality. It was a question of economics.

"Look," said Mick, leaning against the side-board by the sink. "Everybody does it. I don't know one person in my entire circle of friends who doesn't snort occasionally. And look, where do they have to go to get the stuff? To the guys downtown, mostly, and that's not exactly safe."

Archer said nothing, just drank his apple juice and let the boys spout their rationalizations. They were okay guys, he guessed, just a little wired by the sea adventure. They didn't really care about the dangers of drug abuse or drug running. They were just a bunch of Florida kids out for a good time.

Besides, anyone who stocked apple juice in addition to brew couldn't be all bad.

"Well, it's no big thing, you know?" Terry continued. "We won't put a big dent in the other drug pushers, we can get our own stuff, get our own people a quality stash, and make some decent money for our trouble. It's worth it. You know?"

Every three or four months, during semester breaks, they took a plane from Florida to Mexico, and then a train to Puerto Angel. They paid off the Grande Hombre for keeping and stocking their sailboat, then made a quick trip to Guatemala,

Costa Rica, Panama, or El Salvador. They brought it back, refined it in Puerto Angel, and sold it in Key West, Miami, Palm Beach, wherever. Wherever "our own people" need a "quality stash."

It was low-key all the way; hardly a ripple to be felt by hardline pushers and their suppliers. Nobody's nose got too much out of joint. The students figured they could keep this up until graduation day. If the Prof showed signs of creating a dynasty of student drug runners, they could always drop out and let someone else take their places. But for now, everything was copacetic.

And it could get Archer into El Salvador. If he went there by train or by plane there would have to be questions. By the nature of the place now, there would have to be a lot of questions. No honeymooners there now, no curious tourists; El Salvador was not Club Med South. Mucho, mucho pregunta. And Archer didn't want to answer any preguntas at the moment.

"Hey!" Charley called from on deck. "Coffee break over yet? The lovely people of El Salvador welcome you to their beautiful state. Please don't litter or speed. We enforce our laws. That wonderful mecca Garita Palmera just ahead."

"That's our cue," said Terry.

"Hallelujah!" Mick said with relief, scrambling toward the companionway.

The others went after him, Archer taking the rear. His first view of the country was not awe-inspiring: a thin line at the horizon growing dimmer as the sun went down. Bob celebrated by throwing his empty beer can overboard.

"Better make for shore," the Prof said from the wheel. He surveyed dark clouds to the east. "And better drop the jib and reef the mainsail. I think we should make weigh under power from here."

The boys groaned as one. "Aye, Captain," Charley said cheerily. He liked the dark. He liked the damp. He felt a fine, atmospheric, dramatic night coming on for their port stop. The better to load by, he figured. The military and police were less apt to be out on a stormy night.

Archer went along with the others while Charley stayed with the Prof at the wheel. Being that the sloop *John B* was not a racer, the mast was shorter than normal but of a stronger construction and design—as was the rigging. The sloop didn't hoist much sail, which made the whole shebang a lot easier to handle.

Archer partnered with Mick to reef the mainsail so the growing winds wouldn't hurl the boat about as the Prof brought it in under propeller power, while Terry and Bob furled the jib. Mick uncleated the main halyard and Archer cranked the winch that wound the mainsail around the boom.

"Careful of the boom," Terry called from the foredeck. "If the wind catches the sail and the boom isn't secure, it'll swing that thing right into you. If it doesn't crush your ribs, it'll throw you ten feet from the boat."

That's why it was called the boom.

Everyone completed their tasks quickly and Archer felt the motor throb beneath his feet. By then the clouds had moved in, pushing away the sunset-swathed rainbow of sky. Light rain was no more than sea foam from another direction out here where moisture was a way of life.

Unlike the cities, storms seemed natural here. On West Eighty-sixth Street, a cloudburst was a curse. Out here it was organic, an integral part in a larger scheme.

Archer turned his face toward the droplets as the others retreated to the cabin to pull on their dark orange slickers. He saw the coast growing nearer as the Prof pointed the bow toward Acajutla. He didn't want it to end. This had been seventy-two hours of peace, a treaty with the chorea and his more tangible demons.

On that shore, growing nearer, was the answer to a mystery, but one Archer no longer wanted to know. A tiny voice in his gut screamed for him to throw the drug runners overboard and sail away. Sail until the sea claimed him or the Hunter came or starvation brought the big sleep.

Archer tasted a sourness in his mouth and turned to consider the college boys with the designer names on their asses and alligators at their breasts.

He froze in midturn. A speck tugged at the corner of his eye. A raindrop mingled with the fluid there. He blinked, but the speck did not go away. Archer moved toward the stern and peered over the boom. It was a speck, a dark, bobbing speck. As he watched, it became a dot on the horizon between them and the coast.

The dot was getting bigger, and whatever it was was getting closer. Archer called to the Prof, who was manning the wheel with Bob and Charley by his side.

"Hand me the binocs, will you?" Archer asked anybody. He held his hand out until he saw his finger start to shake. He carefully made a fist and lowered his arm. Thankfully, the boat had started to lurch from the slightly heavier seas and no one noticed.

None of the trio moved. But Terry automatically reached for the glasses as he came up the steps from below and handed them to Archer.

"What do you see?" the Prof wanted to know as the dark-haired passenger turned to look toward the shore.

"Shit," said Archer. The word was swept away by the growing wind.

"What is it?" The man responded to Archer's manner, not his speech.

Archer lowered the glasses, his face frozen in an expression of sad disbelief. He was suddenly cold, achey. "What weapons do you have on board?" he asked, turning back toward the men.

"Weapons?" Terry echoed. "What for?"

"What do you see?" Bob demanded, taking the binoculars from him.

"What weapons, Prof?" Archer repeated.

"Robert?" the Prof said, ignoring the question.

"Shit, it's just a motorboat," Bob said, his eyes screwed to the glasses. "No police markings, no markings at all."

"A motorboat?" Charley wondered. "Who's on board?"

"I . . . I can't see anyone," Bob answered. "It must be a fishing boat," he said, turning away. "A pleasure cruise, who knows?"

"They're coming this way," Archer said, "not going ashore."

No one on deck, save one, wanted to believe it, but the Prof had to assume the worst.

"We don't carry weapons," he told Archer tightly. "We can't afford to. If we're boarded. . . ."

It made sense. Weapons would alert any boarder that the crew weren't mere joyriders.

"We have a flare gun," Terry said hopefully.

"I have a spear gun," Mick said, having stuck his head up from below. Archer looked at him. The boy read the *genin*'s mind. "One bolt. I only use it for deep-sea fishing in Mexican waters. After we get back."

"Aw, it's just a motorboat," Bob complained. "Practically a dinghy. Fuck, if you're worried, it's so small we can ram it. It'll sink and there won't even be a scratch on our hull."

"Get to shore," Archer said. "Avoid that boat at all costs."

"It's just a dinghy!" Bob wailed.

"If it's just a local boat coming to warn us about a storm, we could be making trouble," the Prof said reasonably.

"Don't go near it," Archer replied flatly.

"Listen, Jeffries," the Prof continued. "This is your first trip. We've been doing this for two

years. I think we know a bit more about these
waters than you do."

Archer cried inwardly. The Hunter's grip tightened
around his lungs, pushing, pushing. The vacation
was over. He had to move right next to the man to
be heard. When his voice came, it came in gasps.

"It's different. *I'm* here."

The Prof refused to get spooked. Over the last
three days, Archer had lost his edge. All the man
had seen was the Grande Hombre dropping his
gun. He hadn't seen Archer mop the bar floor with
the cop's deputies. Archer held no special power
over him. And with the chorea tightening his
chest, he wouldn't be able to establish any.

"I'm the captain of this ship," the Prof said. "I
don't take orders from you. If you're so concerned,
get below deck. We'll take care of this, hotshot."

Archer struggled down the ladder, the damn
disease nipping at his heels. He forced his balking
legs to get him to his jacket. He jerked it on, only
mildly comforted by the jingle of the throwing
stars in his pockets.

"What is it?" Mick inquired. "What's going on?"

Archer didn't answer. He couldn't, not intelligibly,
at any rate. The words would have come out as
mush.

It didn't make any sense! Why now? Were they
so egomaniacal to think they could track the Ninja
Master from here? Even so, why not wait until the
ship got to shore? Why risk an attack on the open,
lurching seas?

Archer meditated. He forced an instant karma

on himself to calm his tightened nerves. The gravel emptied from his limbs as his mind clawed for the upper register where his killing would come naturally, where it would flow from his body.

Archer swept by Mick and emerged on deck. The dot had become a shape in the rolling seas. The water reflected the sky's colors, turning from a light blue to a plankton-choked green. It changed from clear crystal to a thick, sloppy ooze.

All eyes were on the dark motorboat as it moved toward the sailing vessel. The Prof dared not touch the radio, for fear of alerting the Salvadoran shore patrol to their presence. The rain now cut across the ship in thin sheets, drenching everyone within seconds. The sky had the color of slate. The sloop *John B* surged across the waves toward shore as the motorboat came to within thirty feet of its port bow.

No one could see anyone on board. It was a small, old craft, hardly enough to support two old friends' Sunday fishing. The captain's chair and rear section seemed empty.

"Ah, it's just a dinghy," Bob said with complete conviction, the binoculars back up at his eyes. If so, then why wasn't there a pilot? Jeffries had just spooked them, that's all. "It must've come loose of its mooring and drifted out here."

"I could've sworn I saw the outboard motor running," Terry said.

"Get below," Archer said. "I'll bring us in."

"Shit, Jeffries," the Prof swore. "I told you before—"

"Get down!" Archer shouted, crouching.

Terry and Charley followed his lead instantly. The Prof and Bob watched them with a combination of bewilderment and irritation. How uncool.

The Prof was hit in the chest. Amazingly, Bob was hit in the eye through the binoculars just as he returned them to his face.

It happened between seconds. One second, they were standing. The next, the Prof was crouching, his hand reaching for his left breast. Bob just dropped overboard, falling face forward, his feet slipping back along the slick deck, the binoculars and whatever was holding them to his right eye banging on the hull.

Archer saw the dark brown shaft protruding from the Prof's chest as he ducked behind the narrow coaming. Charley reached for their kneeling captain. The man's eyes glassed over and he fell to his face, sliding under Charley's palm as the boat drifted sickeningly.

The Prof's head slammed into the stern as the shaft was driven through his back, gouging the deck as he slid. Charley fell onto his back and Terry was thrown into the wall. Archer moved to the far side of the ship. Mick was just able to drag himself up to the deck.

"Get below!" Archer instructed. "Terry, you too!" Terry almost buried Mick in his haste to tumble down the steps. "Charley, get us to shore, but keep down." Archer reached up and unclicked the tin box affixed to the cockpit wall below the first-aid kit. From it he pulled the flare gun and three projectiles. He moved around the far wall and up the side of the yacht.

He heard the shot before he saw it. A line stretched from the motorboat to their mast. It grew taut, and Archer saw a figure in black standing on the motorboat's bow, holding the loose end. The other end was affixed to a spear sunk *through* the wooden mast. The dark attackers started pulling the motorboat to the sailboat.

The knife was out of its sheath and through the line almost before Archer knew he had done it. The figure in black on the motorboat's roof fell backward and disappeared. The sailboat jumped forward as Charley revved the motor. More shafts thudded into the deck as Archer slid back under cover.

He looked up and the motorboat was alongside. Another figure in black was jumping from it to the sailboat, like a dark, avenging pirate ghost. Archer jumped forward and swung the boom. Its tip caught the second ninja in the head—home run. The second figure spun in place, flopped across the boom, and fell into the sea between boats just as the waves rocked them together. He was crushed between the two vesseels before he sank.

A third figure grabbed the boom tip and swung it back. It was a vicious, strong push, but Archer was already under it, quickly slinking toward the wheel. The third, emptyhanded ninja jumped on board. Charley spun to face him while Archer slid across the deck, standing upright. As he passed, he shot a flare into the third figure's chest at point-blank range.

Charley had to duck and cover his head as the flare blasted across the man's torso, sending him back in a shower of multicolored sparks. He flew through the air, his chest sizzling, and slammed back onto the motorboat's rear section, bucking and smoking like a living fried chicken.

Archer's smile of savage satisfaction disappeared as a black cloud appeared on the motorboat and threw the flared figure overboard. The cloud then rippled, tore itself into fourths, and came at the sailboat.

Archer reloaded the flare gun and ran to stand in front of Charley. "Get the others and get off the ship," he said, firing the second projectile. It bounded off the motorboat and sank without detonating. He didn't have time to reload the third.

He brought the gun up as an arrow streaked toward his head. It didn't reach his face, but knocked the gun from his hand. These guys were fucking amazing. In the storm, in the night, their aim was this good. Good enough to disarm Archer. Good enough to slam an arrow between Charley's shoulder blades as he went toward the steps.

He missed the steps, his dead body flopping across the cockpit floor. Archer was hurling his *shurikens* before he even had a completely visible target. He only saw vague, moving shapes, but he threw the razor-sharp stars at them.

They reached their marks. They sank in. Archer

felt it in his head, in his heart, and in his soul. That should have stopped at least two. That should have at least *slowed* two. But the figures kept coming.

The *genin* realized they must be wearing padding. The *shurikens* would have to bite more deeply.

Archer spun his body around, his arms seemingly flailing. He tore between the two shapes, his legs swinging in the air. He knew he would have no balance upon landing. It didn't matter. He fell heavily at the stern, next to the Prof's body.

The figure that had been to his right slowed, his arms up to his shoulders. He fell to his knees, face forward, to lie beside Archer. The *genin* quickly stabbed the knife into the ninja's spinal cord, just as quickly as he had slashed in both directions with his knife in one hand and a *shuriken* in the other.

The other figure was wounded but not stopped. He turned, firing the spear-pistol. His wound threw off his aim and the shaft buried itself in the stern four inches from Archer, who knelt and hurled the *shuriken*.

Theirs was not the only good aim. The throwing star embedded in the figure's forehead. He drifted drunkenly to the left and disappeared over the side, swallowed by the sea.

Archer dove for the stairs as arrows dotted his trail behind him. He did not stand on ceremony; he slid on his stomach to the steps and dove down. The final two ninjas came on board. The first hurled glass balls at the deck. They shattered, leaving liquid that was then washed away by the sea waves lapping over the rails. He could not set the ship ablaze.

The second jumped toward the steps, a thirteen-inch *tanto* short-blade in his hand. He dropped below deck. The first figure heard a wet thump. He did not see Mick's spear gun hurl its steel shaft through the second figure's head and into the wallboard. Archer pulled the *tanto* from the man's dead hand and danced back, the spear gun in his other grip.

He stood between Mick and Terry at the rear of the cabin, waiting for the final move.

He cursed himself for a fool, although he knew there had been no alternative. His back was to the wall now, and he had no option but to counter an attack, not initiate one of his own. To put his head up now would be to invite a turkey shoot.

He waited with the others as the ship rocked brutally on the choppy surf. The foodstuffs and beverages tipped over the shelves' protecting rails and smashed on the floor. Mick and Terry held on for dear life. Archer stood with the *tanto* in one hand, the empty spear gun in the other.

They heard footsteps above them.

"What's he doing?" Terry whispered.

They heard a strange cracking.

"The sails!" Mick breathed. "He's raising the sails!"

The motor roared to its highest revs. The ship twisted to the right. Powder erupted from the stairs. Archer ducked and covered, running foward. The other boys' balance was thrown. They stumbled or fell. The figure in black leapt from above deck, catapulting downstairs.

Archer met him there, the spear gun deflecting the spear pistol's aim. The shaft sank into the deck as the powder seeped into the college kids' skin. Mick and Terry started to scream. Archer fought with the figure on the swaying floor, the spear gun his *katana* and the *tanto* his *wakizashi*.

The figure danced as the boys died.

10

Mick and Terry's deaths were horrible. Their screams lanced through Archer's brain as he parried the figure in black's death blows. The ship coursed through the water, the wind carrying it to speeds it had not neared during the past three days.

The boys cringed on the floor, mucus and bile erupting from their mouths, their muscles tightening like dried leather strips. They were thrown from wall to wall inside the small enclosure as the sailboat smashed through the rising waves.

The final figure in black's hands flew through the air. At times they seemed to multiply: four arms, then six, trying to break through Archer's defense. Then they seemed to stretch; arms twice the length they normally were suddenly became rubber, bending at impossible angles.

Archer had to blink, had to try to wash away the false images. The arms couldn't be stretching, they couldn't be duplicating. The figure in black was doing something to his mind. The figure was teaming with the Hunter to cripple Archer's brain.

But the Ninja Master flowed through his *genin*. Five years was enough to give Archer the strength to fight on, regardless. Sixty months of training every day with weapons, books, and computers. But it was more than that. It was his *shihan*'s inspiration, it was his *shihan*'s energy, it was his *shihan*'s aura which flowed through the disease-riddled Archer.

It made his feet find purchase on the tipping floor. It made his legs lash out, holding the enemy off. It made his arms swing through indescribable defense patterns. The figure was driven back into the cabin corner.

The figure threw his arms out and spun. Archer ducked, then leapt up as more deadly powder fanned out.

The spear gun was dropped; Archer used his free hand to grab onto the top shelf in the eating area. He slashed down with the *tanto* just as his feet climbed up the other shelves. For an astonishing few seconds, he was lying backfirst on the ceiling.

The figure's shirt was cut at the shoulder and a thin red slice appeared across his flesh. The powder flicked onto his exposed skin. The attacker gasped and rolled across the floor. He stood, ripping a gallon jug of cider from the opposite shelves. He tore the top off and poured it over his torso. The liquid splashed onto his exposed shoulder.

The figure threw the jug down. When he raised his hands again, a golden needle was between the fore and middle fingers of both fists.

Archer dropped to the cabin floor. His legs gave out beneath him. The Hunter had found him and wrapped him in a bear hug.

It wasn't enough that he toppled to the floor, his limbs jerking as if his head had been cut off. In a way, his head *had* been cut off. His brain was invaded by swirling, laughing images: laughter that mingled with screams; faces, disembodied heads, flying at his eyes as if thrown. The images were imposed over this equally unbelievable reality. It was the hallucination of a brain-swollen child. Archer would have whimpered had he been able to breathe. But the Hunter had tightened his grip around Archer's lungs.

The figure watched, only his shoulders and chest giving evidence of his intent to move in. But suddenly the figure started. His head twisted toward his exposed, cut shoulder. The cider had not been enough to wash away all the poison. He took two steps and leaped up through the companionway and onto the deck. He hardly paused to spin the wheel before diving into the sea.

The yacht swung violently to the left, parallel to the waves. The mast tipped closer and closer to the whitecaps. The wind smashed into the reefed mainsail and the boat began to capsize. Water coursed onto the deck and the keel broke the water's surface. Water poured into the hold and the cabin, submerging the four bodies there. Then the sloop *John B* slipped beneath the waves.

The dragon was at home in the sea. Its camel head appeared first, striped with bright ceramic colors. Its smile was evil and its yellow eyes seemed to glow through the water. It craned its snake neck around, peering at the floating bodies.

Its head shot forward and its open mouth clamped onto Terry's corpse, biting, biting, then swallowing it whole. Archer watched as the body was forced through the dragon's scaly neck and into its clambelly. The dragon shook its head as if pleased. The eagle claws on its tiger's paws appeared and sheathed.

The dragon floated through the water and suddenly bit down on Mick's body. it was all but thrown down the dragon's throat, blood seeping from the monster's lips like octopus ink. Like a shark, the dragon chopped into the dead ninja attached to the wall by the spear. It pulled and ripped at the black-shrouded corpse until the head was torn from the spear like paper from a tack.

The ninja followed the two college boys. The beast was satisfied . . . for now.

A big smile passed across the dragon's face now and then the head changed. The skin began to suck in through its eyes and nose and cow-ears. It left the outline of a skull, a human skull. The excess bone peeled away, creating a necklace of bones about the skull's neck. Steam and bloody mist rose from the skull, which was no longer pleased.

The dragon skin ripped from the skull's great body, a regal body that tore through the ship, sending it all to a great unknown—a thick blackness that was not the sea.

The skull stood in space and spoke.

"What do you want in Mictlan? Why summon me?"

His questions demanded answers. Silent wonder and speechless awe would lead to a horrible fate.

"I know not where I am," Archer thought, his words louder and clearer than speech. "I do not know you."

The skull smiled. Yes, it smiled, with infinite patience. "You need not know me. I am Mictlantecutli, Lord of the Underworld, ruler of the Kingdom of Death. You seek entrance or escape?"

"I do not know. Have I a choice?"

"It is your own. You step on the path to but the first stage. Only in the Ninth Hell is the Eternal House of the Dead."

"You are not here to take me?"

"I do not take; I rule. Beware the face of Tezcatlipoca, for his sorcery and magic lead to night and a death that knows no peace. You come here for rest, yet you do not enter."

"I have fought, but not for this. Yet I yearn for it."

Mictlantecutli nodded sagely. The skull showed wisdom. "Your rest would not be helpful. I may lead you back here yet, but you will have to wait. You cannot enter. Not now."

Archer wanted to speak. The skull stopped him.

"Patience. You can always return. There are eight stages before eternity. You may pass through one. Will that satisfy you?"

Archer woke among the dead.

They were under him, they were beside him, they were on top of him. They bled across his body, they drooled across his skin. They crushed down on him, their bones brittle, their limbs seemingly filled with sand.

And they rocked. They did not lie still, they pushed him farther and farther down toward the Ninth Hell. They rocked, they lurched, they jumped. They jumped in a prone position. Their bodies would be catapulted up, a space would appear between them for a split second, then they would lie heavily across Archer again.

The chorea had fled his limbs. As Jane Phillips has said, after a particularly agressive bout things would improve—and the attack on the boat had been aggressive. He was still contorting when the water hit. It smashed him into the hull wall while his limbs were refusing to swim. He watched himself vibrate in frustration as the sea filled his mouth and nose.

There was no pain. The ocean could not steal his air because the Hunter had already done that. It was the rage that tore at him from the inside out. He would drown because he could not swim.

He knew how to, but his limbs would not respond to his mind's silent screams.

Unconsciousness came hard. It attacked his head with pickaxes and chopped at his struggling form until blackness erupted from his rent skin as if a dam had broken.

Archer awoke several times during this death. He saw light; he felt grittiness on his skin and dampness on his body. He had gone through Mictlan's first stage, but he was not ready for life yet. His eyes opened several times, but all they saw was a milky whiteness with shades of green swimming through it like puff adders.

When he finally awoke, he awoke among the dead. He could talk again, but chose not to. He felt control of his form again. Hair was in his mouth. Dried blood encircled his nose. He pivoted his head to the right. An American stared back at him. His eyes and mouth were open in shock. His hair was greasy and black. He had a cleft chin. Below it was a black collar with a tiny white square.

A priest.

Archer looked the other way. Other heads, other faces, other arms, other legs; he was in a pile of corpses. They stank of feces and urine. Archer used his other senses. Besides the smells and sights, the sound of a truck engine was loud. The vibrations of thick wheels traversing cracked roads came through the mound's base. He was in a truck carrying bodies.

When the truck lurched again. Archer started to

dig his way out of the pile. He pushed and kicked and clawed until he was able to emerge from the corpses like the phoenix rising from its ashes.

His first sight was two dark-skinned men in green short-sleeve shirts and pants trying to climb the truck wall in fear.

One pointed a Cuban FAL rifle at him before the other suddenly pulled the barrel up, chattering angrily in Spanish.

"*Tonto! Tu quere mata el chofer?*"

"*Pero ... !*" the other stuttered. "*Pero ... !*"

"*No muerto!*" Archer shouted, holding up his hands. "*No muerto!*"

The man who had been smart enough to prevent his friend from shooting Archer peered at the young American with wonder before smiling widely and hitting his still frightened associate on the shoulder.

"Hey, *no muerto*, uh? *El error!*" He looked at Archer with pleasure. "Hey, you're not dead, are you, Senor? Not even close."

Archer tumbled out of the pile, onto the floor at the two men's feet. "Not even close," he agreed. His opinion differed inside his head. His brain hurt badly and his mouth felt like the inside of a camel. He had defecated and urinated in his pants, and the dried sea water had made the rest of his clothes feel like zwieback.

The smart guy made the scared guy point his gun somewhere else. "Hey, Senor," he said, leaning down, "who are you?"

Archer had the presence of mind to say, "Jeffries."

"Norte Americano?"

"Si."

The two men looked at each other and nodded. "What are you doing here?" asked the smart guy.

Archer knew the magic word and used it. "Reporter."

The guys positively beamed. "Press!" the scared one cheered.

"Hey, hey, Norte Americano," asked the smart guy. "Where from? *Newsweek? Newsweek?*"

"No, Bristol *Herald Courier.*" Archer didn't for the life of him know why he said that. He read a good article in there once. What he didn't want was too big a paper or newsweekly that anyone could check him out on.

"Ah-huh," the smart guy said, slightly disappointed. "Big paper?"

"The biggest in the Virginia-Tennessee area," Archer said proudly.

"Oh, *big* paper!" announced the scared guy.

"Who are these people?" Archer asked, changing the subject and hooking a thumb at the pile of corpses behind him.

"Ohhh," the smart guy said. "Poor people. Norte Americanos, like you." Corpses were no big deal in El Salvador.

"That's why you in there," said the scared one. "We thought you...ah...muerto."

The smart guy hit him in the stomach with the back of his hand. This was a reporter. *He* was the one who talked to the press.

"Who killed them?"

"Ohhhh." The smart guy tsked. "*Blanco mano*. Death squads. You know? Bad men, oooh, bad men. Far-right government secret police. Kill your people. Kill Salvadoran people. Oppress the masses."

Archer didn't have the mental strength to chew this information yet, let alone swallow it.

"Where are we?"

"On the road outside Sonsonate. We bury the dead."

Archer turned to look into the face of a bearded man. Sudden recognition infused his mind. The priest with the cleft chin and black hair. This man with a beard. He had seen them before. He had seen them . . . on television! These were the Peacemongers!

The memory played before Archer's mind's eye. The asshole reporter marching before the standing troops of Peacemongers, mouthing her somber platitudes while they looked uncomfortable—all but one, all looked ill at ease but one.

Any normal eye would roll right off this one, even on television. He blended in with the others. His edges seemed to mingle with theirs. Even on the sharpest film, he seemed out of focus. He didn't look anywhere in particular, only glancing at the news camera lens for a split second. He had gray eyes, sandy hair. He looked small, nondescript.

He had changed, but he was Brett Wallace.

Archer was on his feet as if propelled. He dug through the pile, looking for any sign of his *sensei*, his *shihan*. As he went from body to body, his mind picked up details. They were all murdered.

It was no accidental death, not even a matter of being caught in sniper or "friendly" fire. Whoever had killed these people had fun doing it.

Bullet holes, bruises, cuts, slashes, knife wounds, cigarette burns. They had been tortured and they had been killed.

Oh yes, two more things. No women. And no Brett Wallace.

"Is this all there is?" Archer demanded, whirling toward the pair.

"Isn't this enough?" the scared one asked with unbelieving mirth.

"No, I mean were there others? Another group of Americans? North Americans. Maybe women?"

"Oh no," the smart guy said. "No women, senor. We would not . . . I mean, there were no women. No, no. Oh no."

"Any others? Men, then."

"No, no senor. Maybe later, though. More later. You want a picture, maybe? We can pile them up; you can take a picture for the cover of your Sunday magazine."

"No picture," Archer said, turning back toward the dead Peacemongers. "No camera. No picture."

He stepped to the open back of the truck. He needed air. He looked out at the passing Salvadoran countryside. The road was little more than a thin layer of asphalt over a gray, dusty track. The road was cut from dense foliage amid a mountain rise. Above them was more thick vegetation, and the drop-off below was also rich with foliage before it emptied into the sea.

Archer could imagine what had happened. Somehow he had drifted out of the sinking sailboat. He had floated to shore. These men had found him there. Thinking him dead—and he didn't blame them—he was put with the others. Now they were heading for some graveyard to inter the Norte Americanos.

Archer shook his head, feeling woozy. He had better get back inside before he fell out. He glanced up the road ahead and stiffened.

A baby was in the road.

A small, bawling child was sitting in the middle of the narrow road ahead, directly in front of the truck.

The vehicle was not slowing.

"Hey!" Archer shouted. "Look out! There's a baby . . . uh . . . *criatura! Criatura!*"

The truck didn't falter, it sped directly at the child.

"*Criatura?*" the scared one said weakly as Archer turned back toward the men.

"There's a baby on the road!" Archer shouted. "We won't be able to miss it. Tell the driver to stop."

"Stop?" said the smart guy as if it were a strange word.

"Stop! *Parada! Dejar!!*' Archer screamed into his face. He could already tell it was too late. Even if he pounded his hands on the cab, by the time the driver hit the brakes, it would be too late.

Archer grabbed the scared guy's FAL and pushed

him away. Before the smart guy could unholster his revolver, Archer pointed the automatic rifle at the floor and pulled the trigger. The slugs tore through the sheet metal and wood and burst the truck's right-rear tire.

Archer was hurled through the open back to go crashing through the underbrush below as the vehicle swung across the road. The driver was either very lucky or very good. He braked, swerved, braked again. The truck screeched sideways for ten feet, then stopped in a cloud of dust and smoke. Its left wheels floated off the pavement, tipping tons of hot automobile toward the still bawling child. But then the truck drifted back to all four wheels, sinking in place.

Archer struggled up the steep incline, using the plants for rope. Meanwhile, the three men in the truck cab jumped out of their doors. The smart and scared guy hopped out the open back. The sounds of gunfire began to pound in Archer's ears. He got back to the road in time to see the driver and his two companions dance an odd jig and fall stiffly to the concrete.

Archer walked toward the back of the truck, his mind numb. He only had eyes for the child. It still sat; it still cried; but on either side of it were feet, feet in black paratrooper boots. The man who stood above the child was dressed all in camouflage except for the beret on his head and the sunglasses across his eyes. He held an M16 with a Redi-Mag.

On his belt was a pouch with three more bullet-laden magazines, a survival knife, a flashlight, a canteen, and several FMK2 Model 0 grenades. Across his back was a long dark wooden staff held by a dark brown leather thong across his front.

He was Brett Wallace, the Ninja Master.

He lowered the M16 toward Jeff Archer and pulled the trigger.

PART THREE

"The very first essential for success is a perpetually constant and regular employment of violence."

Adolf Hitler

11

Archer cringed. He pulled his body in, his arms up. Somehow he wasn't surprised that Brett would try to kill him. Try? Hell, he was as good as dead. An M16 in the hands of the Ninja Master, fired at point-blank range? Open the doors of the Ninth Hell, Mictlantecutli, Yasuru was coming home.

The smart guy and the scared one spun in place as the lead tore through their heads and bodies. They didn't even have enough time to instruct their trigger fingers to contract. They died on either side of Archer, dropping heavily to the road.

Archer stood between them, several seconds passing before he realized he was untouched. It was the applause that first clued him. He didn't think demons clapped when you entered the house of the dead. He was right. As he looked up, soldiers were coming from the hills, cheering.

Archer and Wallace stood thirty feet apart. They looked at each other. Archer couldn't see the man's eyes. His expression was vacant. If he had hung a Post No Bills sign across his face, it wouldn't have been out of place. Was this the man he had traveled two thousand, seven hundred miles for? Was this the man he had gotten the chorea for? Was this the man he had risked death for a half dozen times over?

Vacant expression or not, yes.

Still, Archer had somehow expected more. A smile, a sense of relief, gratitude, appreciation—at least some sort of acknowledgment! The *genin* took a step forward. The *jonin* walked away.

Wallace was met at the juncture of road and bush by the soldiers. They were all dark-skinned, young, and enthusiastic. They had the tight musculature and weary faces of fighters everywhere—especially fighters in a guerrilla war. They surrounded Brett, slapping him on the shoulders and back, addressing him in Spanish. The road hardly seemed to exist for them anymore.

Archer walked slowly toward the crying baby. Once his disappointment had ebbed, the questions came galloping back. The Ninja Master? Here? Now? Like this? Why wasn't he in the back of the truck, dead with the other Peacemongers? How could he be on the road instead, armed and dressed as a Salvadoran soldier?

The man who walked toward him now might be

able to supply some of the answers. He came marching down the tropical incline, dressed like Brett, hauling a Heckler & Koch 32A2 assault rifle in the ready position. He barked out orders in Spanish that somehow didn't carry to where Archer was standing. But the soldiers left Brett and fanned out toward the truck and surrounding area.

The man was ready when he approached Archer. His gun wasn't directly threatening, but his finger was on the trigger and his barrel could be pointed at the young man in less than a second. His skin was tanned, his hair light brown, his eyes the same color and narrow under blond eyebrows. His mustache too was a graying blond, over thin lips and a strong jaw.

"Good work, kid," he said. "You saved us a lot of trouble." He stopped in front of Archer and picked up the baby. "There, there, sweetheart," he soothed. "It's all right now. Take it easy, darlin'. Poppa's got you now. It's all over." His voice was deep and scratchy—very reassuring and comfortable to listen to.

Just when Archer was getting used to his surroundings, something as incongruous as this heavily armed soldier comforting a Central American baby in the middle of nowhere came along to screw up his thought processes again. He looked around to see the soldiers changing the tire he had blown out and moving through the brush below the road.

"Where's his mother?" was all Archer could think of saying.

"You got me, kid," the man replied. "We picked him up in the jungle. His mom must've abandoned him."

The realization dawned on Archer like a lizard crawling up his spine. "You mean *you* put him out here in the middle of the road?"

The man was unperturbed by Archer's tone. He kept rocking the baby, who was beginning to quiet. "I gave the order, but it was Moe's idea."

"Moe? Who's Moe?"

"Moe. Your friend there. The guy who saved your butt when he told me you were okay."

"Moe?" Archer couldn't get a grip on any of this. For a second, he toyed with the idea that the chorea was making him hallucinate again. He had to get a grip on things fast. "Where the hell am I?"

"Oh shit, son." The man laughed. "You mean you don't know? Welcome to the most-used rebel trail from sunny Sonsonate, El Salvador. The guerrillas murder their victims and dump them along this road all the time."

"Who the hell are you?"

"Sergeant Frank Bender at your service, son. Special adviser to the Government Cazadore platoon."

"Cazadore?"

"Means *hunter*, son. Now you'd better come with us. You stink to high holy heaven."

They drove the truck back to town. The canvas walls had been pulled up and the men sat on either side, around the mound of rotting corpses, their weapons pointed outward and at the ready.

"Moe" didn't think this was a good idea. Moe wanted them to drive as far north as they could and bury the bodies when they had a chance. When Bender wouldn't go along with that, Moe suggested that they at least use the corpses as shields; but Bender vetoed that particular idea also.

Now Moe sat in the cab, in the passenger seat, surveying the jungle with beady gray eyes.

"*Moe?*" Archer asked Bender again, both sitting in the back, the baby on the soldier's lap.

"That's what he wanted us to call him," the sergeant answered, his eyes also glued to the hills as the vehicle lurched along the beaten road. "We're not exactly overstaffed, so when he showed up a few weeks ago, I didn't do much arguing. Not when he showed us what he could do."

Archer almost didn't want to know. "What *could* he do?"

"Well, I'll tell you, son. We had a few G's holed up in a house in Izalco, but they had a hostage. Your friend shows up ready for work, even though none of us had ever seen him before. Well, he gets in front of us and starts promising the G's the sun in the morning and the moon at night. To make a long story short, they come out from hiding behind the hostage, then he gets up and cuts loose with his M16.

"Well, it was real John Wayne stuff, just like he did with you. The hostage goes dancing back, and we're ready to kill the motherfucker for screwing up. But then the G's drop over dead and the hostage trots away without a scratch. Shit, after that, I'd call him whatever he wanted me to."

"Moe, huh," Archer checked. "Just Moe? No last name?"

"Shit, son, Moe *is* his last name. 'Dare' is his first name. That's what he said his name was. 'Dare Moe.' Funny name, but it suits him, I guess."

Archer laughed and laughed and laughed and laughed. It suited him, all right.

Daremo was the Japanese word for nobody.

Archer laughed all the way into town.

Sonsonate covered four hundred and sixty-five square miles with a population of about three hundred thousand, according to official government figures. A nice town with its own Mexican-rock radio station and a McDonald's. Archer was finally back in civilization.

Everybody reported to the special military headquarters in town, the one behind the big camouflage-painted metal wall with the words *Batallon Octovo con honor y lealted hasta la muerte—FUERZAS ESPECIALES DE EL SALVADOR* emblazoned across it in yellow paint.

They put Archer in a barracks shower with clean, pressed khakis while Sergeant Bender went to report. After cleaning the crud off and putting the new clothes on, the *genin* reassessed his position. *Shurikens?* Gone. Knife? Gone. Money? Gone. Health? Gone. All he had left of America was the watch. He looked under the tactical covering. The crystal was broken. The hands had stopped on 4:06.

Archer took the thing off his wrist and threw it away. At least he still had his aim. The watch went across the room, its strap flapping, right into a green trash can. Swish. Two points.

He turned and Daremo was sitting on the bunk closest to the far door. His gun was on the bed beside him. He held his stick across his knees.

"Your idea, huh?" Archer said flatly. "Your idea to put a baby on the road to stop the truck?" Daremo said nothing. His face held no expression. His sunglasses were still on. "If I hadn't been there, the child would have been killed!"

The Ninja Master said his first words to his student in almost a year, three to be exact. *Don't be stupid.*

Archer swallowed his rage and frustration and pain. The man was right. He was being stupid, not to mention romantic and maudlin. What kind of life, what kind of chance, did the baby have in the strife-torn country with no family? And by everything that was sacred, Wallace would have stopped the truck if it had gone too far. Wouldn't he? Maybe Archer was being stupid.

But didn't he have the right? After all that he had been through, didn't he have the right to blow off a little steam?

No. Not here. Not now. Not while he was still ninja. Where there was smoke, there was fire. And fire killed.

"What are you doing here?" Archer asked in desperation, cutting away all his extraneous questions while coming forward.

He didn't have to ask how. He knew Brett had come as one of the Peacemongers. He wanted to know what had happened, but he did not need to know. It was enough that Brett was alive and the Peacemongers were dead. That was fact. But did Wallace kill them? Archer couldn't believe that. The Ninja Master had never killed an innocent, even on the verge of madness.

But Archer had to know why his *shihan* had come to El Salvador. It would be the reason Archer came as well. The *genin* stood before his *jonin*, looking over the dark glasses into the hard gray eyes. They did not look back as the Ninja Master spoke.

"For twelve months I have been attacked. Attacked with visions of horror. All I know is that these visions are not emanating from my own brain. They are not being created from my *ki*. Still, they were driving me slowly insane. I had to follow them to their source.

"I saw mirrors, empty mirrors. I looked into them to see evil and saw only myself. I tried to hold onto reality, but it slipped through my fingers. I was only dimly aware of how my behavior was creating doubt within my own *ryu* and the ninja clan. By the time I was beginning to understand the attack, it was too late."

Understand? Archer wondered. What was it Brett understood about this subconscious attack?

"Rhea and Hama were instructed to kill you and disband the *ryu*," was all Archer could say.

"I know," Wallace said quietly. "It was the only thing they could do. I know that now."

All the emotion, all the feelings Archer had for his *sensei* returned to him. There was no longer any doubt or anger. He was the Ninja Master's *genin*, his to command. He fell to his knees. "What can we do?"

"Get up," Wallace said tightly. Archer did so. "We are going into the mountains. The people . . ." Here Brett hesitated. Archer saw the deep, horrid emotion flickering across Wallace's eyes. They were lancing jolts of pain.

"Those men—the male Peacemongers—were killed because of me. I left them when I got here, but it was already too late. I am now part of a platoon assigned to track their murderers and find the women."

Archer couldn't contain his confusion. "But if we find them, when we find them, what possible connection . . . ?"

"No if, no when, no connection. We use the platoon to go into the mountains, to go through the 'Lighthouse of the Pacific.' We use them to find Milarepa."

These were not words Archer could accept. Wallace was using the soldiers to get through the jungle to a specific place of which only he knew the meaning. He had no intention of avenging the male Peacemongers' deaths. He had no intention of finding the women. All he cared about was something called Milarepa.

"Milarepa?" Archer asked coldly. "What is that?"

Wallace had not stirred. He knew what effect his words must have been having on his *genin*. But he could not explain how deep and terrible his agony was. He could not tell the disease-stricken, loyal young man why it was so important to find the place. Because he wasn't certain himself.

"Milarepa," he repeated hollowly. "Church of the Empty Mirror."

The church was not still in the humid night. Its spire reached up to the heavens on the cracked, refuse-strewn, weed-strangled street. Newspapers, Big Mac wrappers, and cola cans rolled along the curbstones like mexicali tumbleweeds blown by the evening breeze. Swirling Mexican music emerged from a radio in a kitchen window somewhere.

They had come through the streets after class, after work, and after much thought. The government had failed them, the police had failed them, and the military had failed them. They felt there was only one other place to turn.

They came to pray, to beg for the return of sanity in their little country. They mocked its officials and complained bitterly, then fell to their knees before the unseen, unknown ultimate power, pleading for an end to their woes and the country's horrors.

The Reverend Cristobal Vincente did his best to soothe his flock. He tried to hold all their pain inside himself so they would not burst. But he too was in danger of exploding with grief and anger. So he too had to pour out his bile from time to time, seeking ears for his congregation's plight. He had to speak. It was his duty.

The pews and fixtures were old. His vestments were worn and faded. The statue of the blessed savior was chipped and peeling. But though the seats groaned and gave when sat on, they were clean. It was all very clean, as well-kept as possible. Vincente considered that his duty as well.

The duties were to maintain the church and all its sacraments. Vincente toiled among the ancient religious papers and books in the large library between his dwelling and the inner hall. He cleaned and maintained everything himself. He never rested. Even in sleep, all his thoughts were of the people it was his duty to comfort and aid.

The young and old alike gathered here to light candles and pray. Vincente did not stand on ceremony; he gave confessionals and sang hymns with his parishioners whenever it was needed. The ancient organ would wheeze its throaty tunes at varied times, as the good Father's strong voice kept pace with the faltering, reedy, hollow singing of the Sonsonate people.

Father Vincente kept working at his calling as if nothing were wrong. But the warnings had been clear. They had come for weeks in anonymous letters, in spray-painted words on the outside wall, and over the clandestine radio station frequencies. He was to stop opening his doors to *subversives*.

He was to stop harboring *Communists*. But this was a house of God. He could not close its doors to anyone.

Father Vincente looked over his congregation now. What subversives? What Communists? There was Rosalia D'Mueno, a first-year university student. There was Carlos Riva, a shopkeeper. There was Maria Guevos, a writer for magazines and newspapers. And there were farmers and factory workers, housewives and harlots. The doors of the church were closed to no one.

The killers came late that night. Everyone in the church knew what was happening the moment the truck ground to a halt outside. By the time they heard the booted feet pounding toward the door, many of the women were in a panic. The reporter, the student, and several others tried to reach the exit.

Instead of flying back and crashing against the walls, the doors drifted open smoothly and the men walked in. The man in front was richly bearded with a thick mustache. He fancied himself Castro by the looks of the chewed cigar in his mouth. He fancied himself Khadaffi by the look of the gleaming blued-metal .45 automatic in his green-webbed holster.

The others—there were eight others—ranged in appearance from a camouflage-covered soldier to a man in a Mickey Mouse T-shirt and a New York Yankees cap. To Vincente's horror, a man in back wearing jeans and a work shirt was carrying a plastic pail half-filled with white paint.

They were well geared up for the endeavor. Guevos was hit in the face with a rifle butt. She fell to the floor and lay motionless. D'Mueno was grabbed, mauled, and hurled back down the aisle. Riva ran forward to help her. He was clubbed and pistol-whipped until his jerking legs stilled.

Vincente ran to the last pew and helped D'Mueno to her feet. She was sobbing. She had hit her head on the seat back and her forehead was bleeding, a thin sheet of red curtaining one eye.

"Please," the priest said, "this is a place of God."

"You've been warned, old man," said the leader, unholstering his weapon. It was as simple and as awful as that. Men in the night with guns, killing whomever they chose, killing whoever spoke against the government or was sympathetic to others—with or without knowing whether the others were Communist. The Castro-clone pointed the .45 at Vincente's head.

There was a whistle and a boom. Vincente was blinded and deafened by the gun blast. When his vision returned, he saw a bullet hole in the pew before him. Then he heard the automatic clattering on the floor and saw a small, dark shape fall after it. Its dark covers fluttered, its pages riffled.

The Death Squad leader's aim had been thrown off by a Bible, a Bible hurled against his hand.

The bearded leader looked up. All the parishioners looked back in shock.

"Who did that?" he barked, feeling foolish. Feeling foolish made him angry. All the churchgoers looked at one another, their mouths silently stammering.

"*Who did that?*"

The people were helpless to reply. Vincente looked around desperately. Suddenly he noticed a man on the aisle, his back to the assassins. At first the priest thought he was a shadow, but then his form took substance, as if Vincente's eyes had focused. He hadn't noticed the sandy-haired man before. And the Death Squad didn't notice him now.

The leader told one of his men to retrieve his gun. Then he demanded they aim their rifles and pistols at the congregation.

"You are all subversives!" he declared. "Enemies to the State. We will question the priest and girl. The rest of you can go to your Communist hell!"

Vincente was aghast. His flock would die, and the girl would suffer the torture of the *Blanco Mano*—rape, burning, teeth-pulling. It was almost too much to bear. He looked to his parishioners in helpless horror. They all stared back, all except the man in black with his back to them. He was no longer there.

One soldier to the leader's side was going to fire first. He had whom he wanted in his sights—a simple farmer he knew very well. His head would splatter like a melon when the bullet hit it. This was going to be very satisfying. That would teach the bastard to throw him out of his house. Maybe after this, he'd go back and visit the man's daughter again—with no interruptions.

The soldier felt a flame fan between his ribs. He looked down and saw something growing out of his side. Another arm was attached to his torso, a thin, round arm. But there was no hand. And the dark arm moved into the shadow of the pews.

The soldier's arm was ripped from his body. It emerged from his trunk and ended in a short stump. Immediately it began to gush blood, then all strength drained from the man's body. He fell sideways, the gun dropping from his lax fingers. When it clattered to the floor, all the Death Squad eyes went to it.

That was the moment.

The word came down from the rafters. The word *was* down.

"*Abajo!*" a voice boomed, and a dark shape jumped among the assassins. They were hopelessly outclassed. These amateur killers, these joy-killing refugees from the streets, were now in the presence of what rightfully should have been their deity. He was the master killer, the lord of the assassins.

Father Vincente could hardly follow the action. The dark-clad sandy-haired figure moved quickly among the center of the squad. His left hand jabbed forward and swung back. A blade went through a man's ear, and the wooden staff connected to that short blade pushed him down.

The right hand swept across the back of two men's necks. The long, straight blade attached to the short dark wooden handle cut through their throats, blood and vertebral shards burbling down their backs.

The left arm lashed out to the side. The long pole with its deadly sharpened blade sank beneath the sternum and into the heart of the soldier holding the paint.

The right hand swept down as the man with the Yankees cap turned to face whatever had jumped into their midst.

He wanted to move forward, but there was something spraying out of his face. His first clue was that his cap visor was cut in two. He only became distantly aware that it was his own blood erupting from the deep cut down his nose and through his lips when he fell back on his way to death.

The Ninja Master slid down, low to the floor. The short blade on the long stick jerked out of a chest and swiveled up into another man's chin. The man with the paint fell, the whitewash spilling across his neck and face.

The blade was in the seventh man's chin. Daremo jerked it up, the sword cutting through the mouth, tongue, palate, and bone and pushing into the brain.

The camouflaged soldier and the leader spun around, guns in their hands. The *ninja-to* stretching from the short handle swung once more, beneath their fingers. Blood from their wrists poured onto the church floor as their adrenaline-driven hearts pumped madly.

The Ninja Master rose to his full height, his gray eyes burning into the camouflaged soldier's vision.

"Dare Moe," the man breathed before he crumpled at the ninja's feet. He had been one of the soldiers in Bender's platoon.

The leader tried to get out of the building. He ran forward, almost knocking into one of his own men. The man stood, his eyes open, dead. He ran around him, almost tripping over a second man kneeling, eyes open, dead. He ran around him while his own blood poured between his clamping fingers, soaking his pant legs.

Father Vincente watched in horror and fascination as the dark-clad man swung the blades toward the floor, wiping both at once on opposite pant legs. Then he jabbed out with the short blade. It disappeared into the rearmost pew. When it emerged, the blade was gone, sheathed in matching wood.

The man swung the longer blade above his head, almost in a parade-leader's showy pattern. A flash, a glint of powerful steel, and then the long blade was slowly sheathed inside the wooden handle of the short blade. The man stood among the corpses, head down, his long wooden stick held to his chest. Only an inch of blade remained exposed. He seemed to be waiting for something.

The Ninja Master listened. The Ninja Master clicked his blade shut.

At that moment, the standing man fell, the kneeling man fell, and the slowing Death Squad leader fell across the open doorway, dead. Not a single shot had been fired. Not four seconds had passed between the time the first man fell and the leader lost his hand.

The Ninja Master stood.

The churchgoers stared for a single second, then ran around him and out the door. Even the wounded college girl struggled out of the priest's protecting grip and ran away.

Within moments, the priest was alone in the church with the unconscious shopkeeper, the nine corpses, and the avenging angel.

"You dare—" He quaked with fear and fury. "You dare make this sacred place a slaughterhouse?"

"Better I than them."

"No better!" Vincente cried. "Different; no better! It is not ours to condemn or punish! You have sinned grievously in the House of God! Thou shalt not kill! Thou shalt not kill!" He fell to his knees, praying feverishly for the souls of the dead.

"No prayers for the living, Father?" the unmoving figure asked quietly. "No prayers for me?"

"I pray for you," the priest declared. "I pray so you may redeem your everlasting soul."

"You *can* do that for me, Father. Only you."

"Leave! Leave this holy place, murderer!"

Here the dark avenger seemed to falter. "You would turn me out?"

Still on his knees, Vincente stabbed toward the door with his right arm. "Go! Go now, before... before others come." The priest turned toward the altar and prayed even more fervently.

"You cannot turn your back on me," he heard

the figure say, close behind him now. "I am one of His children. And I am in torment."

Father Vincente heard the anguish in the voice. He could not ignore it. "What do you want of me?" he asked in pain.

"Milarepa," said the voice. "I seek Milarepa."

12

"There is no such thing as the White Hand."

Bender had to shout it over the roar of the truck.

"No White Hand?" Archer shouted back. "Then who's been killing all the teachers, all the writers.... hell, all the liberals in town?"

The two stood on the opposite running boards of the truck's cab, not looking at each other as they argued. Instead, they watched the darkened countryside go past, ever ready to spot anything human within the packed plant life—if they could see it on this moonless night.

"I didn't say there aren't deaths," Bender maintained. "All I'm saying is that there's no organized, centralized Death Squad headquarters that controls things."

"Sure," Archer countered, "there's only bunches of drunk, power-mad killers running around killing people on whim, for vengeance, and on the express orders of right-wing businessmen and politicians."

"Hey, hey! No politician, no leader of the Salvadoran government in his right mind would ever sanction these things."

"Not sanction. Maybe suggest, maybe desire, maybe hint. Hell, whoever even speaks against the government in passing disappears."

"Okay, Archer. You ever stop to think that maybe the left wing is doing these things? Shaking up the populace, gaining more recruits for their Communist campaign?"

They'd been going at it the entire trip out of town. It was all right with the thirty-four Salvadoran soldiers in the back. It was only humming above the engine noise to them. If anything, any G's who heard the English-speaking argument might shy away, thinking it was the boisterous press corps coming by.

They sat, as usual, back-to-back, their guns facing out of the open rear section, ready and unwilling for anything. Daremo was in the cab, his M16 facing the windshield. Sometimes the G's shot from the side of the road into the cab and men died trying to get a shot out the open window across the driver. Daremo was ready to shoot through the windshield and fuck the glass.

He had returned to camp late at night, telling Bender his network of informants had borne fruit.

The sergeant was plenty pleased to hear that. The higher-ups were pissed about the dead Peacemonger men. And they were pissed about the baby.

When they had unwrapped him from the guy's neck, he told them, not very succinctly, what this was all about.

One, it was not about killing babies. Two, he was down here as an *unofficial* American adviser not attached in any way, shape, or form to the U.S. Government, so he made his own rules (read: mercenary). And three, it was his duty and his pleasure to try to save their butts over this Peacemonger thing, so no shit, please. If he was going to find and/or save the women, he'd have to call the shots his own way.

Shot one: let Daremo do his thing. Shot two: give an M16 to Archer and suit him up so he could replace the AWOL member of the platoon (the Death Squad member Brett had killed without Bender's knowledge). What did Bender know from Hunter's chorea? Never heard of it. Even if Archer had told him about it, it probably wouldn't have made much difference. Bender had a heart murmur. That didn't stop him.

And that didn't stop the two from trading opinions on Salvadoran politics on their way to the "Vol. de Izalco," the westernmost volcano range, otherwise known as the "Lighthouse of the Pacific."

"*Communist?*" Archer echoed. "What a word. What a touchstone. Whenever logic fails, drag that word in."

"Watch yourself, Archer," Bender warned.

"Look, the U.S. promotes agrarian reform, right? That's what this whole thing is about, right?"

"No, smart ass," Bender disagreed, "this whole thing is about Communists trying to take over this country by creating a left-wing revolution and the U.S. Congress getting led around by the nose by a bunch of bullshit artists in the press!"

Archer went on as if uninterrupted. "We give millions, and the Salvadoran Government takes the money, shafts the farmers and landowners, and every liberal—hell, every moderate—who complains winds up with a white hand slapped across their rotting keisters."

"It's all the government, right? The reds and G's have nothing to do with it, right? Big conspiracy theory, right? You hippies love that. You and the *New York Times.*"

"Hippie?" Archer said, aghast. "Hippie? What year is this? You back in Vietnam?"

Archer never got his answer. Daremo signaled the driver to stop and said two words to his *genin*. "Shut up."

Bender leaned down and looked across the driver at his second in command. He nodded. The sergeant hopped down and waved the men out. They fanned out into four lines and moved immediately into the underbrush by the road. Archer hopped off the running board as Daremo emerged.

"There's a path," the young man whispered helpfully, pointing. Daremo brushed by him without a word.

Bender came by with a big smile. "We don't use the paths, greenhorn."

"Why not?" Archer inquired quietly, following the mercenary.

Bender spelled it out as though to a child. "Because the G's use the paths. The G's move at night, so we move at night too. The G's don't use the woods at night, they use the paths. So we use the woods to set up ambushes on the paths. Comprende?"

Archer nodded. He took the tail of the troop with Bender as Daremo led the way. Only Daremo seemed to have any idea of where they were going. Archer wondered if Bender and the Central American boys had any idea at all that their beloved, trusted Daremo wasn't looking for the female Peacemongers.

The *genin* put such thoughts from his mind. Daremo was his *shihan*. He was duty-bound to follow him whatever he did. At the moment, it wasn't that much fun following him. It was an instant-replay of following the Grande Hombre through the Puerto Angel jungle. Branches and large leaves swatted his body.

"Don't these guys believe in clearing the way?" he groaned.

Bender shook his head in amazement. "Let's play make-believe," he whispered. "Make believe you're a G who wants to follow an asshole named Archer and blow his head off. Make believe this asshole was stupid enough to cut you a path through the woods right to him." Bender raised a hand and waved his fingers in Archer's face. "Bye, bye, asshole."

"Why do you even bother to explain these things if they're so obvious," Archer wondered aloud.

"'Cause I don't figure you're gonna be around too long if I don't," Bender said. "Now keep your mouth shut and your eyes open."

It was great fun keeping your eyes open in the dark, walking through reeds and bushes as high as your head. There was nothing to see but chlorophyll and darkness. Occasionally, Archer could just make out patchy clearings on either side, but Brett stayed among the flora, constantly driving the platoon up the steep incline.

It was hot, murderously hot, near the volcano range. The Salvadoran gnats must have smelled imported white meat from North America, because they went after Archer as if it were Thanksgiving. The flak jacket and Fritz helmet only added to his discomfort. By the tenth klick, the seven-pound M16 in his hands felt like seventy pounds; the four grenades on his belt felt like iron balls; and the sloshing of the brackish water in his canteen sounded like a tsunami. At least he didn't have to haul the M79 40mm grenade launchers or the Heckler & Koch sniper rifles. There were three of the former and four of the latter in this Cazadore outfit. The rest of the men carried M16's or FALs with them, along with the grenades, canteens, pouches, and army caps.

They had been walking in the dark for an eternity. They had to be close to something by now. Daremo

never paused or slowed his pace. The others
wheezed to keep up, but none complained. Finally the column slowed to a halt in front of Archer.
Bender just kept walking. He only stopped when
he was alongside the front man, the ninja scout.
Daremo said something to him, and the sergeant
used hand signals.

The men sat down for a rest and a much-needed
MRE—Meal, Ready to Eat—the standard modern
ration. Archer moved through them until he made
a triangle of the Americans' bodies.

"Something's wrong," Daremo said. His gray eyes
moved constantly, trying to pierce the night. "There's
been no opposition."

"Should there be?" Archer lightly inquired. After all, he knew Daremo was leading them on a
wild-goose chase toward a mountain church, not
tracking the Peacemonger women.

"Everything's a trap in G-town," Bender declared,
looking at Brett. "What is it?"

The Ninja Master looked displeased. He didn't
speak. Before the other two could inquire further,
their attention was diverted by a commotion in the
ranks. Two soldiers had jumped up to face each
other, each pulling a blade from his belt or boot.
They looked like cleavers to Archer.

"Shit," said Bender, "that's just what we need.
When these guys get going with their machetes,
you've got to shoot them in the foot before they
know what time it is."

He started to move forward to break it up.
Daremo held him back. The sergeant looked at

him in surprise but stayed back. Archer watched his *sensei* carefully. He had seen him like this before. Still. As still as death. Then, slow, purposeful movement, not wasting a millimeter's space. His head was down, but his eyes were ever-watchful; and his ears carefully edited the night's sounds.

He smoothly pulled the M16 from his shoulder. He held it in one hand. With the other, he fingered a grenade. Archer and Bender very carefully, gingerly, followed suit.

Just below them, slightly down the incline, the two fighters did their silent helmet-dance. The only sounds as they swung at each other were their exhalations of breath as each lunged. The others kept far clear, making a rough circle around them. They were a human boxing ring in which the fighters tried to hack each other apart.

Archer's insides began to boil. Who knew how it started? They were tired, hot, and hungry. A nudge, a bump could have set them off. But now the well-trained platoon's energy was diluted, diverted by the "sport." They had broken ranks and spread out, their backs to the enemy. Archer knew it, but he also knew he could do nothing about it. Telling them to watch out would alert the G's to their presence.

All this could be read on the young man's face. None of it could be read on Daremo's. His head was down, his eyes almost closed, his mouth a single thin line. He watched—or maybe he didn't— the two machete fighters struggle up the hill.

Struggle up the hill? Fighters—blind, angry

fighters—usually traveled the path of least resistance. That was down an incline. To go up it took concentration above and beyond your adversary. Archer saw it; Bender didn't. He was too busy trying to see what Daremo saw, trying to hear what the Ninja Master heard.

The fighters locked arms and made a final lunge toward the commanders. Archer spun and jumped back to protect his *jonin*'s flank. Daremo made an astonishing move, amazing to those who could even see it clearly. With one hand, he brought his staff—the combination *nagamaki/naginata* he had made in the Dawn Dojo's workship from his *katana* and *wakizashi*—off his back. During the same move, it went between Bender's legs. At the end of the move, Daremo twisted the stick.

Bender went down. The machete blade chopped through the air where the mercenary had been.

Daremo shot both fighters with the M16 in one hand. One bullet each, fired so quickly it seemed and sounded like a burst. With the other, he pulled the *naginata*—the short spear—free, using Bender's legs to hold the sheath, spun it, and threw it *behind* him into the trees. He had thrown it backward, not looking in the direction it went.

His right arm hardly moved, but the short blade affixed to the long, rough wooden pole rocketed up through the leaves and came back down with a guerrilla attached to it by his chest.

Already Daremo and Archer were fanning the treetops with their M16's. Bender scrambled to his back and joined them. Men started dropping. Dropping... well, like flies.

They fell from the branches above them like camouflage-colored sandbags, breaking branches and bouncing on the ground. The night was lit by the weapons' flashes; and shell casings ricocheted off balsam tree trunks.

Daremo didn't even try to retrieve his *bo*. He already knew it would do him little good in this situation. He just kept firing in a semicircle up the incline around them. His speed and dexterity were as amazing as Archer would expect. The skills of the ninja did not stop at ancient weapons. The special abilities he had with blades he also had with bullet clips.

The three men flanked each other. Daremo shouted "Clip!" and Archer or Bender would take over while he changed magazines. But the Ninja Master changed magazines faster than the army record-holder. Practically by the time the sergeant had gotten off his first burst, Daremo was shooting again.

The others had reacted almost as quickly as their leader, but they didn't know the enemy's location. Most had hit the dirt and fired to the east, west, or south, but some were caught in the first chopping G salvo. The M60 bullets tore into their guts, and they contorted to the forest floor, blood bursting from their mouths.

Archer and Daremo heard the "whumps" at the same time. "It's raining metal," Archer heard his mind shout before he dove behind the nearest tree. He turned over to see Daremo crouched where he had been, still firing, and Bender rolling down the hill.

The mortar shell blasted above them. The fragments sizzled into the leaves like killer caterpillars. No one was hurt by the first shot, but there were more to come. Many more.

Archer switched clips, and for the first time thanked providence he had the standard ballistic "Fritz" helmet rather than a cap. He tried to get another fix on the enemy's position, but the mortars were now blasting holes all around them.

"Abajo!" Daremo ordered. *"Cava!"*

The men went for their pack shovels and clawed their fingers just as it began to hail lead.

Torrents of M16, M60, and FAL rounds poured into the area, splattering heads, puncturing torsos, and shattering arms and legs. Bender sent the snipers in three directions and unloosed the grenade launchers. They had the M79s in their hands as their eyes sought Daremo. He stabbed his fingers in three new directions.

Each man took one direction with the sawed-off, round-mouthed grenade launchers. Archer heard the "bloop" sound of one sending its bomb out, and the "bloop" of two others going off in unison. They weren't called "bloop tubes" for nothing.

Treetops exploded, clearing a path for more Salvadoran lead to go out and more G lead to come in. The bark and branches spun back at the Cazadores, cutting hands and faces. Bender told them to pour it on; clear a path under the enemy's lip. The bloopers popped their butcher balls forward, tearing up the landscape.

Daremo stood and chopped his arm down, pointing back the way they had come. Bender spun the bloopers around while Moe charged up the hill. He raced past the first G casualty and pulled his *bo* free. Archer saw him disappear into the smoke before following.

Now it really was the Twilight Zone. Archer ran full-tilt through the white, acrid mist, seeing nothing, only feeling the devastated earth beneath his boots. He emerged from the smoke to an awesome sight.

Daremo had found the frontline machine-gun nest. A bunker had been dug above them, and a reconditioned World War Two 30-caliber Browning machine gun had been set up on its tripod. That was what Daremo must have been hearing while the traitors—the double agents—fought.

Daremo had run through the mist, somehow certain that the G's wouldn't fire while their comrades circled behind to cut the Cazadores off. He leapt out of the smoke, over the gun barrel, and into the guerrillas, slicing with the *naginata*.

Archer saw the G behind the trigger as he reared back, his neck open to the bone. He saw the blade dive into the second G's head like a spike going into a melon. He did not see Daremo pull the *nagamaki* from the short-spear's hilt in a lightning *iai* draw, duck beneath the third G's FAL barrel, and cut him open across the chest.

He did not see it because he had already doubled back into the moving cloud of mortar and grenade smoke. He kept running until he dove forward, sliding headfirst to Bender's side.

"Get them out of here. Now!"

The sergeant didn't have to be told twice. He signaled the panic-stricken men to pull out to either the east or west and to kill anything that got in their way. (Swing the arm right and left, then slice it across the throat.)

Archer rolled away, catapulted to his feet, and charged up the hill in a large, upside-down J. Shadows appeared to his right. He shot at them until they evaporated. He arced in toward the bunker and leapt just as Daremo started firing.

Archer soared over the gun barrel, landing at the ammunition box. He fed the hot, spitting machine as Daremo blasted down into the night.

"The guerrillas must've been stalking us for miles," Archer seethed. "Those spies must've fed 'em everything but our shoe size."

Daremo's shake of the head was almost infinitesimal. It was not a vertical shake in agreement, it was a horizontal one. He amazed Archer when he spoke. Not with the eight cliched words he said, but by how he said them: with sarcasm, with humor, with a strange, quiet hysteria.

"There's more to this than meets the eye."

Archer was stunned, but not so stunned that he paused in his work. That would be the last thing Daremo wanted. Daremo must have told his *genin* this as a signal or a warning. The signal was that Daremo was trusting Archer again, that their last five years together had created a bond that was greater than all the horrors visited upon them. The warning was that there were probably more surprises, more shocks to come.

Daremo blasted into the darkness. His eyes seemed to see through the night while Archer's and Bender's eyes saw nothing. Was it his economy and intensity of form that gave the impression that not a bullet was wasted, or was it indeed true? Did each long, pointed shell course unerringly to its human target? Did a guerrilla fall with each round, his skull or chest ripped open?

Many men found out that night.

Daremo fired until there was one ammunition belt left.

"Take over," he told Archer. He waited until the *genin*'s fingers were on the handles before moving forward, racing back toward the Cazadroes' makeshift camp.

Archer watched his *jonin*'s course with amazement. The Ninja Master wasted no words. Instead of instructing Archer where to shoot, he showed him with his body—Archer was to shoot wherever Daremo wasn't.

Archer blasted, concentrating on the task, trying to read his *shihan*'s next move. As he fired, his subconscious taunted him with one thought: was Daremo's warning/signal merely a means to secure Archer's cooperation now? The young man couldn't think about it. By the time the sentence had formed in his head, the bullet belt was empty.

The night was horridly silent as the last echo

died. Archer stood among the G corpses in the hastily built bunker, their bodies still bleeding. The stinging white smoke of the gunpowder swirled around him as he stood in the silent night.

Then he heard the sound of a bird. It was the call of the Japanese auk, the black and white diving seabird indigenous to the orient. It had never been Daremo's signal before, but it was now. It was the *jonin*'s personal signal to his *genin*.

Archer broke the Browning's trigger and took the firing pin out, throwing it away. It was too heavy for the Cazadores to carry, and he didn't want it to be shot at him again. He walked back down to the camp.

He passed the guerrilla corpses. Young men, dark-skinned with dark hair and dark eyes. Some with dark, open eyes. Most in camouflage shirts and pants with black boots. Some with brown boots, some with hiking boots with laces, some with cowboy boots, even. Others with basketball sneakers that laced up to the ankle.

A few had shirts on, T-shirts with American and Mexican designs: Michael Jackson, E.T., Menudo. Most had military caps on, the kind the Cuban army wore, but some had baseball caps. Several were hatless. So these were the men driven from their farms in desperation, driven into the hills by Death Squads and government corruption to join Bender's "Communists."

The bodies did not stop when Archer got back to camp. Only Daremo and Bender stood. The rest sat or lay moaning, their heads in their hands. Archer looked at the sergeant.

"Eighteen K.I.A.," he said. "Six W.I.A."

Funny. Usually the wounded outnumbered the dead. But when the guerrillas had opened fire, the Cazadores had been out in the open. It was singularly amazing that the ten got off with no wounds at all.

"What now?" Archer asked for them.

"We go on," said Daremo.

Now Bender had to balk. "I don't know," he mused. "It's a fucking mess. The G's had us pegged all along, thanks to those traitors. Who knows how many more of them are up there?" He nodded at the ominous shadow of the Izalco volcano looming over them.

"Many more," Daremo said.

Both men looked at the expressionless ninja.

"Shit, Moe!" Bender exclaimed. "A G position?"

The *jonin* didn't bother nodding. Archer walked away in disgust.

"That tears it," Bender continued. "We need reinforcements. We need air support."

"We need a radio," Archer finished for him. He knelt beside the communications man. He was dead beneath his bullet-riddled equipment.

"Then we need a fuckin' battalion," Bender figured.

"A battalion can't get in there," Daremo revealed. "A platoon can't. We can. We thirteen."

The experienced mercenary suddenly became suspicious. "What exactly do you know, Dare Moe?"

Archer faced his *jonin*. He had no thoughts for himself. He was already on the path to death. The Hunter would see to that. "These men did not join the army to commit suicide."

The Ninja Master looked away from Bender's stare, but his clipped, quiet words were for both men. "This country is suicide. This fight is suicide. This is always so when both sides are right."

"What the fuck are you talking about?" Bender exploded quietly. He was as angry as he could get without waking the surrounding five klicks.

Now Daremo looked back at the sergeant. His gaze was cold. "Both sides are fighting for their country with honest intent. Both are fighting for corrupt governments."

"Both sides are right. Both sides are wrong," Archer murmured.

Bender looked at the two men as if they had just turned into six-foot slugs. He looked at one, then the other, his face screwing up as if the slugs had sidled up next to him.

"Let me tell you something about guerrillas, boys," he finally said with pained patience. "They're the same no matter where you are. Terrorists. That's it. Destroy towns, kill people, blow bridges, ruin the economy. That's your 'love of country'? And when it's all over, they're just dupes of the Reds. Communist puppets.

"I don't care what you fuckers say. There's a 'right' here. No matter how corrupt a democratic government is, at least there's hope for change.

You don't get shit from the Reds. Not hope, not faith, not charity. No chance at all."

"When a soldier dies," Daremo said, "it is a soldier who is dead. When a guerrilla dies, it is someone's father, brother, son, or husband who is dead. The death of a soldier makes no more soldiers. Kill a guerrilla, and others take his place."

Bender simply said, "A wise old Communist named Mao once said, 'You need fifteen soldiers per guerrilla.' The way I see it, we can kill five-sixths of a guerrilla with what we've got. Uh-uh, no way, Dare Moe. We go back."

"We go forward," the Ninja Master said. "Or the Peacemonger women will die."

That flattened everybody.

"What the fuck are you saying?" Bender demanded.

This was too much for Archer. The Ninja Master had jumped off his pedestal. Now he was lying to get what he wanted, cursing the Cazadores to almost certain death.

The *genin* marched forward. "That's enough, Brett!"

"What?" Bender wanted to know. "Brett? Is that your real name?"

Archer ignored the mercenary. "I know what you're going through," he said to his *jonin*. "I am carrying your fate inside me. I have the disease meant for you. I know your pain. But you cannot do this. You are putting your life above all others!"

Daremo was frowning; a tight, intense combination of frustration, rage, and sadness.

"The women will die if we do not continue," he repeated.

Bender stepped into the fray. "Why should I believe you?"

Daremo looked at him calmly, his frown gone. "Believe or not. Go or not. With or without you, I shall continue."

That did it. Bender knew that Daremo was too good not to know what he was doing. Daremo was too good to lie. Not to him. If it was important enough for Daremo to go on, and if he said a small band of men could achieve what a battalion could not, then fuck it, the dirty baker's dozen was back in business.

Without a word, Sgt. Frank Bender turned and went to get the others ready.

Archer glared at his *shihan*. Daremo stared back. He was not Brett Wallace anymore. That name was the pseudonym of a man who had died in San Francisco. Brian Williams was still alive, but just barely. And he would surely die if Daremo did not reach Milarepa.

"It is true," he told his *genin*. "The women are there. There is more than meets the eye."

Incredible, Archer thought. Suddenly the young man was more tired than he had been in weeks. He was drained by the surprises, the shock, and the insanity. He looked away. Anywhere but at his *jonin*.

He saw the dead Cazadores. Except for the uniforms, they looked the same as the guerrillas.

An army of children where everybody and nobody was right.

He hadn't known any of them. They hadn't been real people to him before. Who were they? What had they been? Who were their wives, their children, their families, their loved ones? It made no difference. They had been someone once; they were just *daremo* now.

Bender returned with the reluctant ten. "All right, Brett Dare Moe," he said sardonically, "I'm trusting you with my ass because you're the best fucking fighter I've ever seen." The sergeant then leaned in real close. "But I'll promise you something: you get me killed, and I swear, I swear, I'll be taking you to hell with me. Someway, somehow, I'll drag you down with me." He straightened. "Now let's go."

"Yasuru," Daremo said, "start up the mountain."

Bender looked at Archer. The *genin* silently sighed and set off. Bender looked back at Daremo. He stood before the wounded, his *bo* in his hand. The mercenary understood and led the remaining soldiers after Archer.

The Ninja Master turned and walked to where the dying were laid beneath two maquilishuat trees. Their branches' vividly colored flowers were closed for the night, but their perfume filled the air. The dying lay on a bed of their rainbow petals. Daremo spoke to them in Spanish.

"You have fought for a cause beyond anything you know," he said. "You have reason to be proud, and this country—this world—will sing of your courage for as long as it exists. I am eternally in your debt. You will not be forgotten."

And then the Ninja Master killed all six before any of them knew it; quickly, and as much as any living man can truly know, painlessly.

Their severed necks pumped blood while their heads started down the hill, gathering maquilishuat petals as they rolled.

13

They died one by one.

The men that Archer had been so certain would be led to their doom, *were* being led to their doom. Somehow he had convinced himself that Daremo would protect them. When he had seen his *shihan*'s intensity, he had been convinced that he would protect the ten the way he had protected Archer all these years.

Like Hercules who stopped to aid a Roman stranded by a broken chariot, only to refuse to help him when he wouldn't help himself, Daremo could survive, but could not guarantee the survival of anyone with a less advanced knowledge of self-protection—and killing—as he.

The first two died in a sniper attack. The third and fourth died when the M79 grenade launcher mal-

functioned, but it was due to human error. The third
soldier had been given the device when the soldier
originally trained to operate the launcher was killed
during the first ambush. In his haste to blow apart
the treetop where the sniper lay, he blew himself
away instead. *May Mictlan watch over them and
guide them safely to the Ninth Hell,* Archer thought.

The first two men's skulls had popped open at
the backs of their heads. The inexperienced grenade man had whirled around. He had followed
Bender's instructions precisely . . . he thought. He
pulled the pin, dropped the grenade down the
wide mouth of the blooper, aimed, pulled the
trigger, and . . . nothing happened.

He pulled the trigger again as all but one of the
others scattered.

Bender shouted "Throw it!" just as it blew. Hot,
twisted shards of metal sank into the third man's
face and skinned his hands like banana peels. A
piece of shrapnel slammed into the fourth man just
below the ear as he turned to see why everyone
was acting so strangely.

He hadn't heard the silenced sniper's rifle, hadn't
seen his mates fall. One second he frowned and
started to turn, then he crossed the black line,
never knowing why death had come.

Even Daremo waited until the grenade had
blown before disintegrating the sniper. Even he
couldn't judge where every piece of debris would
fly. But as soon as the shrapnel had sunk into the
ground and the bark, Bender fanned the branches
and Daremo plugged the darkly dressed figure in

the stomach and chest. The guerrilla died with five bullets in him, but the wooden fingers of the tree held him aloft.

The fifth Cazadore died when he stupidly broke ranks to get a clear view of Daremo's scouting technique. Daremo was ahead ten paces, checking their path while Bender and the others stayed behind him. One soldier near the middle of the line, tired of looking at his mate's back, stepped to the left to see what was ahead.

What was ahead was a land mine.

Daremo whirled when the small explosive cracked the night, just in time to watch the man's left leg rip open from the sole of his foot to his knee like a bone-and-blood-filled stalk of bamboo. The others crouched and cringed instinctively. The man collapsed, screaming. Bender was up first, his .45 sidearm unholstered and aimed.

He shot the wounded man in the head just as Archer started forward to give aid. The *genin* stared at the sergeant. For himself, the mercenary offered no apology nor explanation. Instead he looked up at Daremo and said quietly, "Mines. That's not like them." He frowned. What had Daremo gotten them into?

Daremo may have nodded, or he may have merely lowered his head. At any rate, he turned and continued up the Izalco volcano.

At six thousand and four feet high, it was certainly not the highest. The Santa Ana volcano had that distinction at seven thousand, eight hundred and twelve feet. But the Izalco volcano was high enough to make legs feel like blood sausages and chests wheeze like rusted furnaces.

The air got thin and the sky got light. The farther they went, the more Archer's head pounded. Sunrise, when it finally came, brought a lightheaded giddiness to the *genin's* tortured mind.

Everyone around him was dying so his sensei *could go to church.*

The desk burst in dozens of little eruptions. Pieces of wood, leather, and felt spun in a pyrotechnical show. The debris spun away, leaving dozens of minuscule metal balls spreading toward his torso. He almost smiled. They shot across the room at him in super-slow motion. They were going to bounce off him, he thought. They were going to tickle.

They didn't. Just as the pellets reached him, they disappeared, and his stomach exploded as the desk had. But this time it was pieces of shirt, skin, and muscle that filled the air. Pain overloaded his senses.

He saw nothing but a milky whiteness streaked with brown, as if his face had been flattened by a marble slab. He heard nothing but a deafening roar, as if eternity were a tidal wave. He smelled nothing but his own fear.

Going there was bad, but coming back was worse. Reality returned with a vengeance. If he had had another second, he could have accepted the milky white, the roaring, the stench of fright, because in it lay an inherent promise of peace. But back in the study, across the desk from Anthony B.

Merritt in the Revenge House, there was no peace, only agonizing pain.

Through the Vaseline-smeared images, he could see someone behind the desk—and it wasn't Anthony Merritt, the corrupt lawyer. The someone was in shadow. But the wounded boy across from the shadow was losing it. His stomach was falling out of his body and into his hands. He didn't have time to face the figure behind the desk. The figure, then, faced him.

It bowed until its face was nearly touching his, a face of hollow, astonishing evil. It had sunken red eyes; a wide, flat nose; thin, bloodless lips; and yellow, snarling teeth. Strips of red were across its chin and cheeks—perhaps war paint, perhaps strips of torn skin revealing the crimson sheen beneath. It was the wet, glowing face of Tezcatlipoca.

Archer's mouth opened to scream. The Aztec face changed instantly to that of a slimy, drooling insect. Archer had no time to study it, for the monstrosity leapt into his mouth and clawed down his throat.

Archer snapped back to El Salvador. He almost cried out in childlike terror. His mind was cracking. The accumulated tension of the ascent was conspiring with The Hunter. As his exhaustion grew, it ate away at his insides faster. It was taking spoonfuls from his mind.

He forced himself to analyze the vision. He had been back at the Revenge House in Cannon Crossing, Connecticut, facing Anthony B. Merritt who had shot him at point-blank range with a hidden riot gun.

The Daremo demigod had helped him who helped himself. Archer had disguised himself as "Tommy Gun" Parker to help the Ninja Master gain access to the place. The Ninja Master had triumphed, killing all the bad guys. But Archer had paid the price with a network of scars across his stomach. He could feel them now.

He fought down panic. What had happened while he was gone? He quickly checked his surroundings. Archer breathed easier. He had not wandered from the pack. While he had flashed back, his legs had kept him with the Cazadores and the sun had come up.

He breathed in the misty morning air, knowing that these few minutes would be the only comfort Central American nature would allow. Soon the sun and the dormant volcano would team up to bake the remaining eight fighters.

But for now, the underbrush was finally lit and something approaching cool. He could finally see what he was swatting. They walked across a carpet of green shredded wheat. Palm bushes were everywhere, as were twisted, wiry trees.

Archer turned to the Cazadore behind him. The man looked farther gone than the *genin* did, but he kept up. Archer smiled supportively. The soldier managed a wan return. Then he nodded, and a fountain of red dribbled out of his mouth and ear. He fell onto Archer.

"Sniper!" the *genin* yelled, dragging himself from under the limp form.

Daremo spun. Bender crouched. And the remaining four Central Americans died in unison.

Twenty-two caliber sniper rifle, Archer thought. Only they could be so effectively silenced that even the Ninja Master couldn't hear them. That meant the snipers had to be close. To be effective, the guns had to fired at almost point-blank range. That meant the snipers had to be practically right on top of them.

The Cazadore quartet spun, jerked, and fell. All three Americans looked for a target. They got one in spades. At least a dozen guerrillas stepped from the bushes. They had not been stalking—Daremo would have heard them; they had been waiting. With all the mountain to choose from, they had guessed where Daremo would come: the path least taken. They held M60's and FALs pointed at the Americans' hearts and heads.

Bender was in shock. Daremo was a statue. Archer looked again to the dead. This was no chance slaughter. The G's had stripped the Salvadorans from around the imported hired help. They would have been happy to get rid of everyone at the first ambush, but now they were just as pleased to get the Norte Americanos alive.

"Throw down your weapons," said a man in halting English.

Bender slowly laid his assault rifle on the matted forest floor. Archer dropped his like an unwanted present.

Daremo didn't move.

"Throw down your weapons!" the same man

shouted, jabbing his own gun in Daremo's direction. The three men closest to him also shifted until they were aiming directly at the ninja. Well-trained, thought Archer.

Daremo slowly lowered the M16 butt to the ground and leaned on the barrel like a cane.

"Dejar callo!" the man shouted. *Drop it*. It seemed he was only instructed to say "Throw down your weapons" in English. He let off a burst in Moe's direction. The bullets gouged the earth inches from the man's feet.

Daremo didn't move.

For a second the man wasn't sure whether to get really angry and shoot Daremo dead or let him keep his damn rifle. But it was quite obvious he was under instructions, so he controlled himself and found a compromise—the compromise Daremo was silently suggesting to him with all his considerable inner energy.

"Bah!" said the man. He instructed the three closest to Moe to take the weapon from him and kill him if he tried anything.

As they approached the still-motionless, seemingly casual *jonin*, his eyes moved, his eyesight pinioning his *genin*. The *genin* looked to the mercenary. The message was clear throughout the remaining Cazadore ranks: he was going to try something. When the something was tried, the others were to do what they could.

The men came over to Daremo. They pushed him away from the M16 with their rifle barrels and took the gun. They turned back toward their leader in triumph. Daremo's arm went out and he threw something that whistled as if it were slicing the air.

It was a sound Archer knew well: a *shuriken* thrown so accurately that it could light a match.

Archer saw it all in his mind's eye: the *shuriken* in the leader's forehead; the others stunned for a second; Archer and Bender killing them all in a chopping cross fire.

That almost happened. Archer was already reaching for his gun when he heard the throwing star hit its target. When he came up firing, he didn't bother shooting at the man he thought was already dead. When he came up, Bender was firing behind Archer. Archer returned the favor by firing to the sergeant's side.

Daremo's *nagamaki*, his *ninja-to* in its new housing, came out of the hollow *naginata* staff in a lightning *iai* whose first cut was part of the draw. It slashed through all three spines of the men who had disarmed him. But before they fell, he pulled his M16 from their dying hands and shot the leader between the eyes.

Archer saw the leader's expression of shock as the tiny red hole appeared at the bridge of his nose and his head jerked back. He fell while the *genin* wondered. If that man hadn't been Daremo's *shuriken* target, then who... or what...?

"Run!" the ninja called. "This way! Quickly!"

Bender and Archer covered his rear. Daremo was running as fast as he could away from the spot, while the sergeant and the *genin* covered his tracks. They were being military; they were not following his example.

"Forget that!" he shouted. "Just run!" His logic, and target, became immediately apparent.

Archer followed his *jonin*'s orders. Bender was reluctant to turn his back on the enemy. He watched as several guerrilla survivors took aim. Bender brought his gun up to stop them. But then they dropped their FALs, screaming. They danced like epileptics, slapping their faces.

Bender's eyes widened, and he ran as fast as he could.

Daremo had thrown his *shuriken* into a wad of loose, beige netting he had seen under a fallen tree some fifty feet behind the guerrillas. He had recognized it for what it was: a nest of the infamous South American—now Central American—killer bees.

Despite the jokes, these insects were real and the terror of all woodland farmers in the region. They swarmed, they attacked, and they protected their low-lying hives up to a hundred feet away.

The horror for the guerrillas was that they knew what had hit them. As they felt the powerful stings sinking into their skin, they had to live (and die) with the knowledge that the bees' poison was slow and cumulative. And that the creatures swarmed hundreds at a time; once in their midst, there was no escape.

Daremo's savage logic was sound. He could kill the leader; Bender and Archer could kill some of the others; but there was only one way to get them all. Kill the leader, get some others, and let the bees take the rest.

The only problem was making sure the bees didn't get *them*. And the only way to make sure of that was to put a lot of distance between themselves and the buzzers. Since Daremo had someplace specific to go, it wasn't much of a problem. He charged directly for a hole in the side of the mountain.

It was not a gaping cave opening, just a small crack in the rock face, easily missed by someone even passing close by. You had to move to the right, beside a vertical outcropping, then bear left to get inside. The three Americans ducked in.

They stopped ten feet beyond the opening. Already the darkness was deep. They gave their eyes a few seconds to adjust.

"More guards?" the mercenary hissed.

"I doubt it," said Daremo. "Their forces are probably concentrated near the larger volcano openings."

Bender unclipped the flashlight from his belt and illuminated the scene: damp, warm walls; low ceiling; narrow tunnels. They were inside the dormant Izalco volcano. Outside, the screams of the stung were finally dying out.

"This is it, isn't it?" Archer asked. "Entrance to Milarepa."

Daremo nodded.

"And we don't go step one until I know what I'm in for," said an angry, gasping Bender.

Daremo started to walk deeper into the cave anyway, but he spoke quietly while he did so.

"The women were taken to a village called Milarepa," he revealed. "They are being used as rewards."

"Rewards?" Bender exclaimed. "For what?" he wondered, then answered himself. "Shit. A training camp?" He didn't have to see Daremo's nod. "Oh fuck," he groaned. "Why didn't you let me call in a battalion?"

No answer was desired or forthcoming. The sergeant already knew that the bulky army would have never gotten through; they would have been spotted immediately and hacked up piecemeal by hit-and-run G bands. The Cazadores had been almost able to slip through because their unit was so small. Thirteen men attacking a training camp was insane, so naturally they almost made it.

"What?" Archer asked.

"The much-vaunted, legendary terrorist training camp, hotshot." Bender groaned, breathing heavily. The walls were beginning to close in. The floor was littered with rocks and branches. The sergeant was having a hard time keeping his footing. He shone the light on the floor, but it was strangely barren.

"Turn that off," Daremo snapped. He didn't want their entrance telegraphed. The place was heavily guarded enough. From his talk with Father Vincente, he had hoped to find a secret, undiscovered entrance. No such luck, but at least it wasn't mobbed by guerrillas.

Bender returned the light to his belt and filled in Archer. "The Cubans are bankrolled by the Soviets to train the G's in the fine art of murdering Americans," he continued tightly, almost sickened by the thought.

"They're thoroughly trained in the best KGB style, sent to the U.S. as students or waiters or whatever, and Uncle Sam pays them unemployment and welfare while they make bombs to plant in offices, schools, churches, airports, and train stations."

Then the sergeant sang a little tune. It was the chorus stanza of Billy Joel's "Only the Good Die Young," but he cut the line short. "Only the good die," he choked.

The full weight of the horror fell on Archer. "Oh God," he breathed. "The women were sent *there*?" He remembered their faces from the newscast: caring, kind American faces. The represented the best the country had to offer. They were the meek who were supposed to inherit the Earth. What person, no matter how meek, would want *this* Earth? The cruel could keep it.

Archer looked into the darkness to try to see Daremo's face. He had been in control all along. Which came first, Archer wondered, the women or Milarepa? Had he found the church while tracking the women, or found the women while tracking the church? Did he somehow know the Peacemongers were going to go there before joining them, or was it just a gruesome coincidence?

Did it make any difference anymore? Not really. Archer had to accept the situation for what it was. But his addled mind wanted—no, make that needed—to understand.

"Why here?" he asked the darkness before him. "Why now?"

Daremo wanted to tell his *genin* to think. He did

not want to have to spell it out. But he remembered what his thoughts had been like after the
first needle. Archer had gotten the second. Although
the *jonin*'s mind still burned with horrible images,
he had controlled them. He could distinguish
between them and reality. Archer had the more
tangible nightmare of The Hunter in his veins.

"I was led here," he said simply.

Archer did not so much think of him as see him
in his brain. The figure in black. The Ninja Master
had stalked the figure in black, and that monster
had brought him here. That monster had left clues
where Daremo could find him. And the more
Daremo researched and reconnaissanced, the more
he came to believe that the Church of the Empty
Mirror held an antidote to his anguish.

That was why *here*. That was why *now*. But still
there remained *why*?

The question seemed a tangible block, making
the going even more difficult. The walls closed in
ever tighter, and the steamy heat grew. Bender felt
his legs slogging through something, as if walking
through piles of confetti. He had ducked when the
darkness of the ceiling had loomed down, but he
had not physically felt it. He did so now.

His arms sank into the ceiling up to his elbows.
He stretched his arms out. They sank into the
walls up to his shoulders.

And the walls and ceiling moved.

Bender brought his lamp up and flicked its
switch. All three men were in the light. And all
around them were cockroaches.

Cockroaches, some half a foot long, were covering the walls of the volcano tunnel. They were piled on top of themselves, crawling across themselves, always moving. They were two feet thick on every tunnel surface.

Daremo and Archer seemed to be struck down by the same hand of god. They reeled as if drunk. Archer actually fell to one knee, the cockroaches coming up to his chest. The only thing that saved him from being swamped by them was the light. They ran from light. In a matter of seconds, the space in the flashlight beam was clear, completely clean of the insects.

Daremo rolled his head on his neck and fell, his mouth slack. He fell heavily to his side, the *bo* and M16 clattering on the ground. Archer crawled to him.

"What happened?" Bender cried, his own equilibrium shaken. First the claustrophobic cave, then the bugs, now this. "What's the matter with you two?"

The face that looked up at Bender was not the Archer he knew. It was not the man he had argued with on the truck or shepherded through the wood. This was a haunted shell.

"We sshaar tha sssime nighmah," Archer's mouth painfully shaped. *We share the same nightmare,* he had tried to say, but the Hunter had attacked his mouth. The Hunter was crawling up his spinal cord to clamp onto his brain.

Daremo's vision cleared. "You see?" he said, eyes closed. "You see now? We were led. The images, the nightmares . . . they were not coincidences, they were not false perceptions from our own consciousness. They were visions. They were guides. And they were warnings."

The words jabbed at Archer. It just wasn't possible. Psychic control? Could someone, something human, invade his mind?

Daremo's eyes snapped open. They were clear. He looked upside down, on his back, deeper into the tunnel. The cockroaches were receding like a tide going out, running from the light. But in their midst, mountains were beginning to form.

"*Onis!*" he hissed, vaulting to his feet, the M16 swinging into his hands. He blasted into the insects, hunks of their crackling shells splattering the walls.

Bender lunged forward, thinking the man insane, until he saw the blood spurting from the insect waves.

Men were rising out of the bugs.

Daremo had called them "devils" in Japanese, and he wasn't far off. They were camp guards lying in wait under the cockroaches. They wore suits that covered their entire bodies. Their heads were covered by hoods that attached to the necks of the outfits, and their eyes were covered by infrared glasses. They hauled Soviet Kalashnikov AK assault rifles in their mitts.

Fucking shit on toast, Bender thought. If those guys let off a burst in these cramped quarters, the good guys would be dead before the echo started. Bender pushed his weapon beside Daremo and pulled the trigger. Both men emptied their guns into the sea of cockroaches in front of them. The blasts were so loud in the tunnel that they didn't hear Archer's screams.

Most of the words were unintelligible, but "No" and "Don't let them get me" could be made out if anyone was in the mood to listen. Then The Hunter gagged him and wrenched his puppet strings sadistically.

Bender glanced over his shoulder to see why Archer wasn't helping. Archer was on his back on the cave floor, spazzing out.

He drooled, rolled his eyes, and shook. And the cockroaches were beginning to cover him.

Bender knew what he should have done. He should have kept firing at the mounds rising from the cockroach ocean in front of him. But he saw one of the bugs scurry into Archer's mouth. He couldn't stand any more. He had not brought the young man this far to have him drown, have him choke, on cockroaches.

He turned, reached down, and dragged Archer to his feet. The young man couldn't stop shaking. The flashlight beam wavered, and in it Bender could see shapes growing *behind* them. The G's had crawled through the bugs, under the insects behind them as well.

Bender threw Archer behind him, between Daremo and himself, and pulled his trigger. Click. Empty gun.

Bender hastily changed clips as the dark red suits began to appear between the insects. He jammed the magazine home, brought the barrel up, and pulled the trigger—just after they pulled theirs. He blasted them as he felt three 5.56 bullets drill into his stomach and intestines.

They were aiming blind, covered with cockroaches,

so they didn't kill him. Besides, he was just a
shape in the infrared. He had no such problem.

It was a bizarre shooting gallery. Daremo and
Bender back-to-back; the tunnel illuminated by
the jagged flame from their M16's; Archer convuls-
ing on the ground between them.

Men and insects died. The thunder of the guns
sounded like an avalanche in the narrow tunnel.
Hunks of flesh and bugs slapped into both the
ninja's and mercenary's faces. They emptied one
clip, then a second, then a third into the swirling
mass of cockroaches. They fired until the pile of
insects grew no more mounds.

Daremo turned when Bender collapsed. The
sergeant had dropped to his knees. A terrorist
exploded from the cockroaches in front of Daremo.
Archer pulled the *nagamaki* from its sheath and
held it so the last attacker was impaled.

The Hunter had been defeated yet again. Archer had emerged from the seizure in time to save
his *jonin*. The final body-suited storm trooper
stood, the *ninja-to* through him. It took him several
seconds to realize he was dead before collapsing.

Daremo returned his attention to the sergeant.

"Don't mind me," Bender joked through clenched,
bloodstained teeth. "Just a scratch."

Archer slid over to the mercenary while Daremo
retrieved his *nagamaki*. Blood spurted across his
camouflage suit when he yanked the blade free.
Archer used the flashlight beam to chase the
cockroaches off Bender's body.

"You're going to take care of it, right?" he said to

Archer. "I mean, whatever's wrong with you guys, you're still going to be able to take care of business, aren't you?"

Archer nodded with little conviction.

"It's important. I wouldn't ask you unless it was important." Sweat had covered the mercenary's face like a kabuki mask. He was hot to the touch, but getting colder. "Good ol' Unca Sam has El Sal's ass in a sling over this one, okay? A couple of nuns is one thing, but a dozen U.S. citizens, and Peacemongers to boot. I mean, Congress'll go apeshit, right?"

"Right," said Archer. Daremo stood to Bender's side, the long silver blade still in his hand.

"You guys all right now?" Bender asked the *jonin*, his voice a whisper. His arms were wrapped around his middle. Blood was drooling between them, soaking his sleeves.

Archer looked to his *shihan*. He nodded. The worst of their nightmares were past. The worst of their reality was to come.

"We'll take care of things," Archer promised. His voice was steady.

Bender looked at the odd scene: two crippled assassins and one dying mercenary in a hot cave full of cockroaches and corpses in science-fiction suits. The sarge shook his head and laughed. His expression afterward said it was a mistake.

"Shhh," he exhaled in a snort. "So this was what it was like when the dinosaurs died. There's no place for warriors anymore, good buddies. The U.S. is afraid of its own power. They can't afford to have warriors anymore."

He looked up at the ninja with pure envy. "You understand, don't you, Dare Moe? You had a whole warrior class once, didn't ya? This was what it was like when the samurai class was wiped out, isn't it?"

Daremo paused, then nodded. Bender looked at the cave floor.

"Yeah, I know," he said with wistful pain. "I've seen those swords advertised in magazines. Nothing like yours, though, I bet. I read the articles about modern *ninjutsu*. But you guys aren't fucking around. You're the real thing, aren't you?"

"Yeah," said Archer with aversion.

"Okay, then," Bender said, pulling himself up. "I won't keep you. Just a second."

Daremo quickly yanked Archer aside. The *genin* marveled at the ninja and the mercenary's silent understanding as he slid to the cave wall.

Bender suddenly whipped out his survival knife from his boot and buried it in his stomach up to its hilt. He pulled it across, through the bullet holes, blood bursting into his lap like an undammed waterfall.

He was committing seppuku, the warrior class's ritual hara-kiri. A noble hero's death. The cockroaches didn't care. They charged him.

"Do it!" Bender hissed.

In one graceful, powerful stroke, the Ninja Master cut his head off.

It flew into the darkness and sank in a mass of insects. Sgt. Frank Bender's body was a fountain of crimson liquid. It fell forward. It was soon covered by a carpet of cockroaches.

Daremo said a Japanese prayer. Yasuru cried.

14

The death of Sergeant Bender brought only despair. The *shihan* and his student were not having much fun to begin with, but the mercenary had brought a grim vitality to their quest. He had sought to find some justice, some truth in the seemingly nonstop brutality of this tiny Central American country.

El Salvador was hardly as big as Vermont. The Ninja Master had only seen a few square miles in a few short months, and already the relentless inhumanity was paralyzing. Bender's endeavors had been honorable. With him gone, the quest—so near its end—seemed anticlimactic.

The *shihan* and his student waded through the cockroaches dressed in the dark red suits of the guerrilla storm troppers—the hoods over their heads, the glasses over their eyes; high-tech, New Wave ninjas, Soviet AKs under their arms. Daremo moved smoothly, but Archer had a strange, dancelike gait. The Hunter had been subdued, but now he moved in. His tentacles stretched across the *genin*'s every bone.

They emerged into the sunlight upon a wooden platform. Stairs led down thirty feet to the ground. To their right and left were other platforms at similar openings, and on each of these platforms stood guards.

Each was casually dressed in the garb of a mountain guerrilla—the usual T-shirt, camouflage shirt, or dress shirt. And each held a rifle or submachine weapon. All were pointed at the two ninja.

Below was a natural amphitheater, carved out of a volcanic plain. It was perfect. Not only couldn't Bender's precious battalion reach it without a firefight, but the air support he had mentioned couldn't deliver a killing blow either. It was nestled on the back side of a volcano.

There were two guard towers on either side, and two barracks between them. Closest to Daremo was a long, low building, that looked as if it could double as a schoolhouse and town hall. Along the edge of the encampment were replicas of traditional American city buildings: restaurants, retail stores, police stations, fire stations, a library.

And in the middle of it all stood an Aztec church. It had two dusty brown levels, rising up into a roughly pyramidical shape. The entrance was on the second level, up at least twenty-five steps. It was simple and barren and out of place among the elaborate preparations for war.

Daremo felt its *ki* just looking at it. But the darker

ki of something not so powerful but more pressing distracted his concentration. He looked down.

Standing at the base of the stairs were a young man and young woman: he dressed in an Izod shirt, Levi jeans, and Nike sneakers; she dressed in a sleeveless T-shirt with a red sun emblazoned on it, a pair of Calvin Kleins, and high-heeled Candie's sandals. They both wore sunglasses.

The ninja was faced with the American dream gone haywire.

She held a Tokarev 7.62mm automatic. He held a small, bulky black box on a gunlike handle. There was a dial on the back and a patch of tight silver netting on the front. It looked like a hand-held portable stereo speaker.

"Welcome to Milarepa," the young woman said.

The young man pulled the trigger.

Archer was astonished when Daremo fell down the stairs. But suddenly he no longer knew where he was. It was an acute sensation of disorientation. It was like The Hunter, in that he no longer had control, but it was not his body that revolted while his trapped mind screamed. It was his mind that degenerated while the body wondered what the fuck was going on.

Archer collapsed in an ultimate state of confusion. He wailed for Mictlantecutli to watch over him. He screamed at the thought of Tezcatlipoca. But all he heard was laughter.

When he awoke, the *genin* was much more inclined to believe in the possibility of psychic attack.

He was dizzy for a few seconds, then nauseous, but that too soon passed. He lay in his T-shirt and camouflage pants. He was in a windowless, long, low room—so low, in fact, that he could not stand up. His boots were gone.

"Sound waves," a voice said. "It reproduces the exact pattern of the electronic impulses to your brain at the base of your spine. It jams them, the way you can jam radio waves. The brain is cut off from all input."

The voice was melodic, warm, and female. Archer turned over and looked at the owner of the voice.

Her face was wide and bumpy, her body the same. Her hair was dark, parted in the middle, and greasy. She wore a loose, thick denim dress that reached her calves. She had on Dr. Scholl sandals.

"My name is Carol," she offered. "Who are you?"

Archer didn't answer right away. He looked around. They were inside a box. Behind the police station front, a long rectangular crate had been built before the women had arrived. They were housed in this while smaller boxes were built behind the other fronts to serve as detention centers and "coolers" for the least cooperative.

"They don't use the fronts for training," Carol told him. "They had them shipped in specially, but the teachers didn't see any need to accustom the trainees to American locales. Outsiders aren't unusual in the States anymore."

She told him that the Peacemongers had been detained at their hotel one day. They had been directed to two special buses, one for the men and one for the women. They were ambushed on the road into town. They never saw the men again.

"What happened to them?" she asked.

Archer told her.

She shrugged. "It figures." Their corpses weren't real to her. After all, she hadn't awakened lying under them.

Whoever had set them up was probably trying to track the Ninja Master, Archer reasoned. "How long have you been here?" he asked.

"I don't know. A month. Maybe two. No real way to tell." They had stripped her of jewelry and molested her a bit; but the head student, the one who had "greeted" the *genin* and his *shihan*, declared that they would save her—"the sow," they called her—for last. After they had used up all the others.

"I saw their faces the first few weeks," she remembered. The women's faces had looks of disgust, then shock, then tortured agony, then rebellion, then resignation, and finally this glazed, dead look. "I cried when I thought of myself that way. But otherwise I just played 'the sow.' Soon they were using me for all sorts of odds and ends.

"Whenever one of the girls was sick, I nursed her. I nursed a lot. They do things to them . . . to us." She shuddered. "The men are bad, but the women are worse. Especially the Queen Bitch." Their other "host."

So Carol kept her mouth shut and her eyes open. She was unofficially given the job of mother hen: serving meals to the others while under guard, tending the others' wounds, et cetera. Now she knew almost everything there was to know about the compound. Except one thing.

"I've never seen the teachers. Everything I know comes from the Queen Bitch, the head student—the Valedictorian, I call him—or the guards." She talked a blue streak. She poured out everything she had been saving up for the past week or month, or two months or whatever. Finally she grew silent and distant.

"I don't think they'll rape me," she suddenly decided. "I think that when graduation day comes, they'll just slit my throat and leave me with the others." She thought about it. "Yeah, they've been spoiled by the other girls. They'll just kill me and leave. What do you think?"

Archer thought about Daremo. He was alone in the box with Carol. Where was Daremo?

He sat sat cross-legged in the stifling heat, his eyes closed. Long, wrinkled brown fingers touched his face. The old blind mystic of Milarepa considered his subject.

"They came years ago," he said in Spanish. "They drove my people away and destroyed our tiny village. They meant to use this place for ritual sacrifice, as it was in the days of old. But those young people who they brought here would not allow it. Then they meant to kill me; but again the young Aztecs would not allow it."

Daremo ignored the sweat that coursed down his face. Was this the only place to put him away from his *genin*, away from the Peacemonger women? Or did they unconsciously respond to his psychic "suggestions" to put him here? Daremo had used *aisha* before when he had been Brett Wallace. Some call it hypnotism or post-hypnotic suggestion.

"You will let us through. . . ."

"I will let you through. . . ."

Whatever the reason, he was there. He was inside the "temple box" with the mystic who had not left the cramped, fetid enclosure for many years. Food was brought to him. He defecated in a hole in the corner. He urinated in a cup. He drank his urine.

"They thought it a bad omen to kill me. I would stain this place with my spirit." The old man giggled, a delighted, low-pitched cackle of mirth. "Modern children," he mused. Then he turned his blind eyes to Daremo. "But they were right."

The old man was not wasting his words. He was not babbling for want of company. He had felt Daremo's *ki* as soon as the dazed man was thrown inside. Daremo, in return, had felt his. His aura was powerful, but serene. He was at one with his universe. He was the person Daremo had traveled across the continent to see.

Daremo's own aura was fractured. The man was telling him what he needed to know. He was applying the mental salve necessary to follow medicine.

"You are scarred in soul and body," the holy man said. His fingers touched Daremo's chest and arms. His mind's fingers touched Daremo's brain. "You seek something tangible yet intangible."

The room with no walls, floor, or ceiling.

"You seek an answer and a solution."

The difference between the two was immense.

"You seek the empty mirror."

Daremo did not want to see his reflection in evil.

The old man sighed and sat down. "Meditate," he instructed. His *aisha* was strong. Daremo's lids closed like fire curtains.

"Time has seven Sons. Each Son is an Age. The first was the Night Son: the Age of the Wild Cat. The Earth was in darkness, and wild animals roamed free. If a human appeared, it would be eaten. Horror was then visited upon this planet by the Nameless Son: the Age of Famine. All the beasts died and the humans who remained changed into apes.

"They lived until the Earth Son: the Age of Giants. Mountains rose from the ground then crashed into the sea. Behemoths were born and then died. The planet tore open and the only ones who survived had wings or could grow them. They flew through the sky, over the Fire Son: the Age of Lava. The globe was a ball of flame.

"The Air Son brought calm in the Age of Clouds. Humans prospered and built, feeling their power for the first time. The Air Son did not want the people like the gods, so there were whirlwinds and hurricanes that swept the image of humanity away.

"Then came the Water Son and the Age of Judgment. The flood came, killing all the humans save two. But they were changed to dogs when the water subsided. And as dogs they roamed the planet, worshiping the gods as the Sons of Time meant them to.

"The Fifth Son finally appeared, bringing with him the Age of Elements. He had two hands, both closed. We must now choose one of the hands. In both are four elements. In one: Earth, Fire, Air, and Water. In the other; Earthquakes, Famine, War, and Confusion.

"Some say this world will survive because the four elements are balanced. I say the balance can only be maintained if humanity strives not for survival, but for perfection." His blind eyes did not waver, but his whole being seemed to look into Daremo. "You are fighting for your life, not for your perfection. You feel flawed, so you claw for existence."

The holy man was not going to keep the ninja waiting. He would not demand worship or reverence as all false prophets do.

"You are not flawed. Humanity is not flawed. You do not wish to see yourself as you are. You pray for weakness, for therein lies an excuse not to seek perfection. You are like all men, a perfect combination of good and evil. You cannot reject one for the other. You must live with, and accept, both.

"You do not fight for your life. Life is already yours. Your battle is within yourself."

It was graduation day. If the Cazadores could find them, dead or not, others could find them as well. It was time to send the students to America, fold the tents, and slip off into the night.

Archer heard the rain thudding into the top of the box. Carol sat next to him, her knees up to her chest, her arms wrapped about her knees.

"The bugs'll join us tonight," she said. "Get ready for a fun evening."

Daremo's eyes rose as the heavy, tropical raindrops hit the temple's ceiling.

"The Sons are arguing," said the old man. "You will have your answer tonight."

They came for both men in a matter of minutes. Carol was sent to tend the horded, frightened women inside one of the barracks. The graduates had been celebrating with a final taste of American girls. The Queen Bitch held her automatic on Archer, standing six feet away from him outside the police station mockup.

"There's no reason the boys should have all the fun," she decided. She made Archer lie on his back in the mud. Two men pressed the muzzles of their rifles against his chest and forehead as the girl took off her designer jeans and sat on his hips.

So much for sex. Archer performed admirably, considering the circumstances. The Hunter was lulled into inactivity.

As she hauled up the tight denims to her waist, she smiled. "I hope I get pregnant," she said. "I'll think of you during the abortion." Yes, this was one committed terrorist, all rightie.

The holy man's back was turned from the door when the Valedictorian came for Daremo. He hit the ninja with the sound-wave weapon immediately. Daremo had to be dragged out by two guards. The Valedictorian wanted to say something threatening to the old man but somehow could not. His inability to deal with, or kill, the man was infuriating. He marched out of the tiny enclosure, promising to take out his anger on the American men.

They were brought out to the grounds, between guard towers. Above, the Sons argued with heavenly brilliance. Black clouds rolled through each other, moonlight streaking their edges. Water fell in sheets. The fifty students (forty-two men, eight women—they felt more women could always be recruited in the states among the ranks of bored, upper-middle-class sluts) gathered under the school house's lip, wearing yellow slickers from the tops of their heads to their ankles, and rubber boots.

Daremo and Yasuru were drenched in a matter of seconds, their bare feet sinking into the red volcanic mud. They were brought before the Valedictorian and Queen Bitch, who stood on the house's covered porch, training the wave-gun at the captives' heads. Both men had to be held up. No one was taking any chances.

"In a matter of days," the Valedictorian told the others in Spanish, "we will all be in America. We will communicate with these." He held up a replica Sony Walkman. "But only in emergencies. Otherwise you know what you must do."

Hardly a *summa cum laude* speech, but no other details were needed. Each had been instructed in how to create the most terror possible. Not just bombings or kidnappings this time. They would commit murders, mass murders, seemingly motiveless crimes that would continue to point out to the American people how corrupt and ineffective the judicial, legal, law-enforcement, and journalistic establishments were.

The cops would take too long to catch them, if at all. The lawyers would try to get them off, and occasionally succeed. The trials would drag on for years. The psychiatrists would argue. And if convicted at all, there was better than a seventy-five pereent chance they would spend the rest of their days—until possible parole—in far greater comfort than they had been in before their crimes. Psychiatric hospitals were far more opulent than the Salvadoran hovels they had lived in.

And throughout the entire process, the asshole press would champion them, demand their attention, explain their plight, barter for their stories, buy the book rights, buy the television rights, buy the movie rights. The more extreme the crime, the better. Oh yes, these darlings were ready to go.

They had been hand-picked as the most cunning psychotics in the country, people dedicated to self-preservation and others' torture and death.

"To consecrate this occasion," the Valedictorian summed up, "we shall have a ceremony. Death to the gringos!"

"*Death to the gringos!*" the group chanted.

The Queen Bitch aimed her automatic at the back of Daremo's head. She wanted to save Archer for last.

"Death to the anglos!" The Valedictorian shouted.

"*Death to the anglos!*" the crowd boomed.

Carol watched from the barrack's window, clutching Daremo's *bo* to her breast. She thought it was a walking stick and she thought it was Archer's. Big tears rolled from her eyes.

The Valedictorian handed the clumsy wave-gun to a guard and took his revolver. He wanted the men to be just coming aware when they died. "Count!" he shouted.

"*Uno!*" bellowed the crowd just as the wave-gun shattered and the guard collapsed, a gaping, bloody hole in his right leg.

Some got to *Dos!* before they realized that bullets were streaming into their midst as if the Aztecs had returned to take back their land.

The Valedictorian looked up at the volcano, and a bullet went into his right eye. The Queen Bitch instantly dove behind his falling corpse and tried to shoot Archer in the head. He ducked—not because he had eyes in the back of his head, but because it was his instinct upon coming out of the fog.

Archer kept low while he checked the area. The boom behind his head spun him around. The Queen Bitch took aim again. She was five feet away. Archer dragged down the guard next to him with incredible strength. She shot the guard in the face. Archer flattened his own face on the ground as hunks of the guard's head passed by.

Her vision was clouded by a fuzzy, light shape. She screamed when Daremo's fingers sank into her eyes.

It was the trident, one of the most gruesome forms of ninja retribution. Brett Wallace had used it once on a mother-killer before the man could also kill the woman's baby. It was supposed to be used only if mortally wounded as a final show of disrespect—two first fingers in the eyes, thumb in any nostril, squeeze until the eyeballs burst or the fingers touch the socket bone.

Daremo threw the Queen Bitch to the mud. Archer reached over the dead guard, aimed the man's gun at the writhing, screeching female form, and pushed down the guard's trigger finger. The Queen Bitch flopped in place as the point-blank slugs tore her middle up.

"The abortion's on me," Archer thought savagely. But he stood and actually said, "I want them all dead!"

"No," said his *jonin*, moving back on the porch as the bullets ripped up the ground. The students had run for their own guns. "We must find out who their teachers were."

"They're too dangerous!" Archer maintained, leaping to his *shihan*'s side.

"You don't cure the disease by eliminating the sores." Daremo was firm.

"Don't talk to me about disease!" Archer flared. He looked up toward the mountain. He could pick out only two flashes of gunfire near its base Only two. "Yamabushi!" he hissed.

"Yasuru," the Ninja Master warned, looking in the other direction. Archer turned to see Carol running out of the barracks with the *bo* in her hands. Both men ran to the edge of the meeting-house porch and leapt.

She was shot in the right shoulder and left hip. She twisted, and dove to the ground. The wooden staff flew out of her hands. Daremo grabbed one side in midair with one hand while Archer grabbed the other in both. They pulled.

The *nagamaki ninja-to* was in Daremo's grip. The *naginata* short-spear was in Archer's. They ran for the barracks.

Fifty students.

Eight were killed on the campgrounds by the attacker's bullets.

Forty-two had made it to their barracks to get their guns.

It was a low, narrow enclosure. There was only a five-foot path between the two rows of beds. Each terrorist kept an assault rifle and sidearm by his bed. They grabbed for the weapons and moved back toward the doors. Was this their final exam?

Archer went for the door to the right. They were already streaming out into the yard, their eyes scanning the mountain, looking for snipers. What they weren't looking for was a wiry, brown-haired young man in a wet, skintight camouflage shirt and pants swinging a *naginata*.

He would have to move among them. If he got more than a few feet away, they could shoot him easily. The trick was to spin the spear vertically by his side and horizontally over his head, or horizontally *through* them. He paused, waiting by the barracks wall until their congestion was at its apex.

Daremo went through the nearest window. Like his previous jump, this leap looked effortless. It was *karumi*, the light skill. He was in midair, his legs tucked beneath his torso as he erupted into the enclosure. A woman was to his right, grabbing her rifle.

Kesa-giri, the diagonal cut, across her neck. She fell back onto her neighbor's bed, blood tracking her trail, her throat opened.

Daremo landed on the mattress beneath him. A man was at the foot of the bed, bringing his gun up. *Karumi*, over him. *Kiri*, downward, into his skull.

Blood spurted up where Daremo had been. He landed on the bed across the aisle. One man stood to his right, one woman to his left, another man at the bed's headboard.

They expected him to bounce. They all fired up where they thought he'd be. He sank onto the bed with one knee. *Sampo-giri*, the three-direction cut across his chest, across her chest, then *tsuki*, thrust into his chest. *Then* he bounced into the aisle, between two groups, not even aware of his attack, running in opposite directions.

Jumonji-yari, the intricate high and low spinning blade pattern, Archer cutting through the swarm. He had waited until they seemed ready to dissipate. Thirteen students, firing a base volley toward the mountain, ready to move toward the mountain entrances' stairs.

Kesa-giri, through two kneelers. Through one head and through one neck. *Morote-zuki*, the two-handed thrust, immediately into a man's chest. Then pull out, hard, spin, *morote-zuki* into another's back. Plant feet, pivot, pull and swing across two more chests. The second man died. The first fell back wounded, trying to stem the spurts of blood.

They were aware of him now. They stood, turning toward him. Vertical spin, *uke-nagashi*, deflecting an AK barrel, *tsuki*, back kick, toes across an attacker's face, spear pulled out, *tsuka-ate*, striking with the blade handle, in solar plexus. Blade swung down vertically across face. *Sampo-giri* across the kicked man, across the *tsuki-ated* man, into the wounded man.

No pause, no rest, no power posture. Vault over lying man, *kesa-giri* across throat, *jumonji-yari* deflecting their aim. Then quick, quick! *Tsuki, kesa-giri, morote-zuki!*

The last three die.

Gammen-ate, the face thrust.

The man in front of Daremo dies screaming, contorting as he falls slowly to his knees, then to the floor. *Kesa-giri* to the right, *kesa-giri* to the left, while still moving forward. *Morote-zuki* through the back. Out, the man falls, cut with the *ninja-to* across the neck.

Daremo marched through the line heading toward the far door, coming up behind the students and killing. He was nearing the opening where the crowd became denser. *Jumonji-yari* with a dance. Daremo danced, his legs deft and elegant. His arms chopped with an incredible power—no energy wasted. The blade did not catch in the bodies.

Cut skin. Cut muscle. Cut bone. Dance. Watch the dance and die.

The bodies peeled from around Daremo like

scythed sugarcane. The people at the other end of
the barracks became aware of the commotion down
the aisle. They turned to see blood spurting,
bodies dropping, and a gringo harvesting.

They thought not an iota of their comrades.
They raised their rifles.

Feet slammed into the first two's back. They
were slammed to the floor. Archer stood on them,
kesa-giri, *kesa-giri*! Behind them, facing the others,
deflecting their barrels, cutting their faces and throats.

The first two squirmed beneath his feet, trying
to roll, to get up, to fire their guns.

Tsuki down into the one beneath his right foot.
The one beneath his left pulled free, rolled onto
his back and fired.

Archer was no longer there. The man shot three
of his comrades, three comrades who would have
killed Archer with their rifles had they lived.
Instead, *soete-tsuki* into the shooting man's neck.

Archer blocked one exit, Daremo the other. The
students ran from them, learning the terror of
terrorism. They ran toward each other. The *jonin*
and *genin* chased on their heels, striking as they
ran. They met in the middle, three terrorists
sandwiched between them.

Daremo: *kesa-giri*, right.

Yasuru: *morote-zuki*, left.

A final female terrorist remained. She screeched
in fear, the gun unable to find a first target. It shot
the floor.

Nagamaki in her neck.

Naginata in her chest.

15

Daremo stood at the crown of Milarepa.

Archer had started shaking just as the last student died. He could not even pull the spear free, his shakes were so bad. Daremo knocked him unconscious almost immediately. He carried the limp form of his friend across the empty, corpse-strewn campground and up the twenty-five steps to the holy man in the church cell.

"You have won your battle, I see." It seemed a funny thing for a blind man to say.

But Daremo agreed. He had accepted himself. He had accepted whatever conflict he was now involved in. The nightmares had become dreams—visions and warnings—as he had said; not something to be feared, but something to study, to seek to understand.

"But this man," Daremo said. "His body fights him."

"Disease," considered the holy man. "Put him down." The blind Aztec priest's remaining senses were extraordinary. He touched Archer with a combination of acupressure and western medical techniques. He sat back, considering the young man's prone form with empty, white, pupilless eyes.

"I can do something for him," he finally said, "but he will have to remain . . . for a time, at least." The way the old man spoke, he already clearly knew that Daremo must leave, in fact, *should* leave.

Daremo grinned. For the first time in about a year, he really grinned with unpolluted mirth and relief.

Hama and Rhea were waiting for him at the base of the church.

She held a silenced MAC Ingram 11 SMG in her hands. He had an HK PSG 1 counter-sniper rifle—one of those new five-thousand-dollar models—in the crook of his arm. They wore *shinobi shozokos*, the ninja uniform. Their swords were on their backs and their hoods were around their necks. The thinning rain washed their faces.

Daremo considered the sniper rifle, one of the most accurate in the world. "So it *was* you," he said simply and walked toward the second barracks. He did not have to ask why. Daremo was ninja, not to be killed by the enemy in battle. If execution be his fate, then the clan must do it.

The woman and warrior-priest followed the *jonin*—the *ex-jonin*—just like old times. They deserved Daremo's respect, if not gratitude. To successfully launch their attack, they had to march through heavily guarded enemy lines and go *over* the mountain. Then they had to kill every volcano tunnel guard silently, one by one.

They walked, the man with sandy hair and the camouflage suit flanked by black-garbed assassins. They carried guns. He walked with his wooden stick.

In the second barracks were the weeping Peacemonger women. They huddled around one bed. On it lay Carol. She was bandaged, and breathing roughly but deeply.

Daremo stopped abruptly in the doorway. The ninjas almost bumped into him. He looked down, grimacing, almost as if ashamed to look at Carol with her dress off. But then he seemed to shake it, and he marched toward the women with a reassuring smile.

"Don't worry," he told the terrified, quaking female mass. "It's over now."

His right foot anchored ahead of him. The staff came up. The *naginata* cover was off. The spear shot across the space in a blur.

It sank into a woman's head as she was bringing up her Tokarev automatic. It fired into the ceiling and she dove back like a comedienne slipping on a banana peel. She slammed onto the floor, her arms and legs wide as the real Peacemonger women scurried away, shrieking.

Daremo looked at Hama with a grin. "I traveled with these women, remember. I knew there was a face here I didn't recognize." Not to mention the women's manner. Weeping over Carol was one thing. Crying in shivering fear was another. They knew Daremo. Why show such fright when the battle was over? They should have been still numb from shock at the students' graduation orgy.

He told them to collect their things. He told them to stay by their beds. He told them they would be taken out of here and no one would hurt them again.

Big deal. They were already hurt enough for two lifetimes. Daremo couldn't help wondering whether any would ever truly recuperate from this experience. It wasn't for him to decide or know, so he forgot it immediately. He went toward the last student's body.

"Don't bother," said Hama.

Daremo looked at the placid Japanese, then stooped to pick up the *naginata* cover. Hama was unimpressed. In the *jonin*'s fist that way, it could be used as a *kubotan*, but what could a measly *kubotan* do against two *ninja-tos* and a combined firepower of 17mm?

They went outside. The rain had stopped and the sun was beginning to rise. It was a beautiful day for a beheading. They stood between the church and the meeting house.

"Kneel," said Hama in Japanese.

"Fuck you," said the Ninja Master.

Rhea gasped. Daremo grinned at her.

"Kneel!" Hama barked, gravel in his voice.

"Forget it."

The silence was charged with electricity. The *yamabushi* didn't know what to do, his rage was so great.

"The *shihan* was right!" he bellowed, pointing. "It was *ki-chigai* to accept a white man into our clan! Insanity!"

It was Daremo's turn to be unimpressed. "I'm ashamed of you both," he said conversationally, with just a tinge of disgust.

"Of *us*?" Rhea choked.

"First, when the warlord goes bad, it is the clan that commits seppuku."

"That is samurai Bushido," Hama growled. "We are ninja."

"Very good," Daremo considered. "You've learned your first lesson. You're not executing me because of clan rules or clan honor. You're executing me because you think I pose a threat to you." Rhea opened her mouth. Daremo cut her off. "Or, in actuality, *someone else* thinks I pose a threat to you. You're just doing the dirty work." He shrugged. "Why not? Ninjas are good at that."

Hama's mind backed up and went into another gear. "I see you're all better," he said casually.

"And I'm not going to roll over," Daremo promised. "I *am* ashamed of you. You're taking someone else's word about me. You are judging me without seeing any of the evidence yourself."

Hama snorted. "I saw all I had to in San Francisco."

Daremo snorted in return. "Erratic behavior. That's your conclusive evidence?"

It was working on Rhea. All along she had been doubting the *shihan*'s claim of Daremo's disloyalty and treachery. "Yamabushi," she said, touching Hama's arm, "perhaps . . ."

He pushed her away. "No!" He turned to Daremo, his sword off his back and in his hands. "The ninja do not have Bushido, but they do have honor and they do have a heritage. A faith. I will not, I *cannot* turn my back on it!"

Daremo glanced at the ground. When he looked back, his face was flecked with disappointment and resignation. "No rituals now, Hama. If you're going to kill me, it'll have to be with your blade or your bullets. And it'll be messy."

"So be it," said Hama, coming forward.

Even Daremo's arms could not block a samurai blade. Hama moved in fast and chopped down. The *naginata* sheath broke in two.

Surprise. A *third* blade—a squat, short blade— was secreted at the base of the *naginata* sheath. *It* could block the samurai blade. *Uke-nagashi* and off. The two men clashed and separated, walking around each other like caged tigers.

"Shoot him," Hama told Rhea, who stood to the side. He couldn't go for his own gun. In that split second, Daremo would move in. "Shoot him!"

Daremo did not act smug. He did not say "Save your breath" or taunt Rhea with her own helplessness. Instead he told her what Hama was unable to hear. He would listen, but he would not hear.

"Don't," he told her. "We were attacked in California—all of us, not just you. They attacked your bodies, but they attacked my mind. I still don't know how they did it—microwaves, hypnosis, psychic assaults—but I know they did. I was led here and I will be led elsewhere. Whatever is happening here is not over, not even close."

"You see?" Hama shouted. "You see? He admits

it himself! He is being used! Shoot him! Shoot him now!"

Rhea was crying. There were no tears, but she was crying. She loved him, but she had to believe that white men were weaker than orientals. Although he would not want to, he would succumb to whatever force was tugging at him. And he would not run from the danger. He would march into its jaws. She knew him too well.

She loved him.

She had to kill him.

The gun came down off her shoulders and into her hands. Then she went down.

Daremo thought she had collapsed. Hama saw his opening and went for it. The blade of his *ninja-to* just touched the *jonin's* shirt when the *yamabushi* also fell.

His oriental *genins* lay in the mud, motionless. Their backs rose and fell, so they were alive, they breathed. In his present mood, Daremo considered that they might have been swatted down by a psychic hand. But then a dreamlike memory came to him. A figure he had only met in a previous life. A figure in black.

Daremo looked slowly over his shoulder. The figure in black emerged from the meeting house.

"*Chugoku-jin,*" Daremo said. Chinese.

The Chinese. It was not just ninjas who sought to destroy the Wallace *ryu*. In fact, it was only Hama and Rhea who represented the Japanese. Their ancient enemies, their neighbors, were playing one against the other like master musicians. The darting, black-garbed figures were Chinese. The figure in black...? Their leader?

He walked out, the blowgun in his hand. More gold needles, no doubt. He did not respond to the ninja's accusation. He opened his fingers and let the blowgun drop. It was a simple two-foot-long tube.

The two men faced each other, just as Daremo had faced so many others in this, his age of darkness—his lover, his judge, his *genin*, himself.

He looked up at the volcano. It marked this age and his emergence from the night. In its honor, he named it. It was his season of lava.

"You have been testing me, leading me," Daremo said in Chinese. "You confront me now. Why?"

"I have been *using* you," the figure said with a laugh, his voice a high Mandarin chant. *"Bair nan ren,"* he taunted. White man. "You are the ninjas' last desperate hope. And you *will* be the means of their destruction."

The figure had said nothing Daremo had not already suspected. He was the first, and only, round-eye trained in the Japanese secret arts—the only white man, at any rate. Why had he been trained? Out of pity? The poor Caucasian with the dead pregnant Japanese wife? Don't be stupid.

"You have not answered my question," he told the figure.

The figure ignored it, but used Daremo's words as a springboard for his own. "You are truly *daremo*. You are nothing but a pawn in our struggle, our thousand-year struggle to destroy that which *we* created. *Ninjutsu* sought to kill its creator and escape. There is no escape for *ninjutsu*, not through their stolen skills and not through you. I will prove you truly *nani mo, shiroi ninja*. You *are* truly nothing, white ninja. They sought to use you to escape their fate. But I shall make you their fate. I shall make you our puppet. I will show you our superiority . . . your nonexistence."

It was a smoke screen. The Chinese had failed here. They had trained the terrorists well, trained them to be even more insidious than the Russians could have, but now all their students were dead. There *was* more here than met even the Ninja Master's eyes. How did rapists and killers in America tie in with the Chinese *Moshuh Nanren*?

Moshuh Nanren were magic men, the infamous magician/ spies who brought their killing talents to Japan in the first century.

They had dogged the *ryu*'s trail. They had tried to keep Archer from his *sensei* while keeping Hama and Rhea unaware of their presence. That was why they had attempted a seafaring attack. They led Daremo unerringly to this place. To kill? Doubtful. To taunt? Definitely. And perhaps to actually subjugate him, as the figure had said.

The Ninja Master rubbed his chin, then swept his hand over his face as if cleaning off the figure's words. Then he put both his hands up to his chest and casually motioned the figure to "come on."

They charged each other.

Daremo tried to snake the *naginata* surprise blade in, but the figure had snakes of his own. He was trying for a devastating, all-inclusive win. Incredibly, his left arm was utilizing snake-style Chinese kungfu while his right was tiger claw. The two forms flowed across his upper and lower limbs until they became a devastating new form of snake claw.

The blade was ejected from Daremo's hand with brutal force, his chest battered, and a final claw went across his face. The ninja used the powerful, scratching swipe as a catapult. He hurled his body back and to the side, spinning in the air.

The figure followed in *hung gar*, the careful style that judged the ninja's movements and struck down as Daremo tried to get away. One vicious blow to his spinning side convinced him to find his feet. Daremo catapulted up, and the figure landed a devastating blow to his back. A straightforward, powerful karate kick.

Daremo had to fall again. If he had tried to fight back or resist, his back would have broken. The figure seemed intent on not only defeating him, but humiliating him. He used the dizzying variety of styles not because he had to, but because he wanted the ninja to see just how outclassed he was.

But still the figure did not let up. There was no second taken to gloat. The beating was insult enough. The figure dove in and drove white-crane beaks toward Daremo's body. The ninja's feet came up, knocking the hands away with a speed and dexterity that took the figure by surprise.

Daremo's fingers, in their own beak, pecked at the figure's bended knee. The figure's hands went for protection and attack. Daremo's leg lashed over the arms, cannoning the figure back.

This time Daremo was the one who offered no respite. In spite of his bruises and wounds, he catapulted to his feet and came after the shaken figure. They met with swinging fists, variations on the *Choy-Li-Fut* style. Their arms clashed, their knuckles swung just short of their targets.

Kungfu is not an art of death. It is an art of *not* being killed. At its base, in its origins at the Shaolin Temple (in China), it was meant as a self-defense mechanism. It is not the art of hitting. It is the art of not being hit.

In the first few brutal seconds, Daremo had accumulated enough information about his opponent—and remembered enough of their first horrid confrontation in the flaming dojo—to counter the blows. Their arms now locked and their legs continued. It was basic *Chang Chuan* style, the foundation of Chinese kungfu. But in Chinese kungfu, nothing was truly basic.

The figure used his incredibly pliant joints to assail Daremo with feet and knees. Daremo could only counter, each block really a blow to less vulnerable areas. Just because the blows rained on his calves and thighs didn't mean there was no pain.

Daremo slammed his head forward. There was no block for that. The figure reeled back. The blow even staggered Daremo. He too stumbled. The ground between them ripped upward.

Daremo looked to his left. The Peacemonger women had come to the barracks door. One held a smoking assault rifle. Her face said that she too was amazed. Daremo looked back at the figure with a tired, pained smile.

The figure read his mind. "They can't kill me if I'm next to you!" He charged again. The woman fired, but the bullets went behind the speeding figure. He was a dim shape in the sunrise, and the woman was not an experienced shot.

It was *Wing Chun*, the short form. Tight attacks on the enemy's center line. One-inch punches.

Block, block, block again. And again. And again. No room for attack. No room to move forward. The figure was a bulldozer with spears for arms and clubs for legs.

Daremo ran backward. Literally ran, his own hands a desperate blur in defense. It was not enough. Fingers, like blunt knives, connected constantly.

They were behind the school house now, blocked off from the women. Wham. Two palm sides smashed into his sternum and ribs. Daremo jumped back. The figure jumped forward. Wham. Fingertips at the base of his throat and in his solar plexus. Wham. A foot, an anchored leg sending the side of a foot across his face.

Daremo fell onto his back, nearly unconscious. The figure fell with him. The figure wrapped his legs around Daremo's and knelt, locking the ninja's limbs. Two knife hands, fingers like blades, slammed into his shoulders where his arms connected to his chest. Those limbs were now paralyzed.

His head came up, his teeth clenched, the veins standing out on his neck. The pain. The pain. The vision: the figure's arms were back; the fingers, claws. One of three things: a killing blow to the throat, a killing blow to the skull, a killing blow to both. There was only one thing those three blows had in common.

"The women cannot save you now!" the figure howled in triumph.

Daremo rolled his tongue and exhaled sharply.

The figure leapt back, absolutely stunned. There was a needle stuck in the side of his hand.

Daremo smiled at him. Between his teeth was a tiny plastic tube no bigger than a needle itself.

"We meet again," Daremo said.

Brett Wallace had been wounded with a needle. Jeff Archer had been wounded with a needle. Now Rhea and Hama had both been hit by needles. Daremo had sworn that when he and the figure in black met again, he would be ready.

It came back now, the image of Daremo rubbing his chin and face just before fighting. After that, there had been no more words. He had slipped the tiny tube that had been affixed in his sleeve— the tube he had first actually secreted in his sphincter so his captors wouldn't find it—into his mouth, and under his tongue.

The figure did not know what was on the almost bee-stinger-size needle. It could be anything. The ninja, true to their origins, were masters of poison. The figure ran.

"It is not over, *shiroi ninja!*" he screamed. "Your clan has not yet answered for its crimes against the *Liu-chias!*"

The women came hesitantly around the corner of the meeting house as the figure reached the Aztec temple. Daremo rose quickly to his feet.

"Give me that," he said impatiently, grabbing the AK from the woman's hands. To the accompaniment of incredible pain, he whirled and fired. The bullets chopped up the ground, ricocheted off the tan granite of the steps, and tore bark from the trees. Not one hit the figure in black.

Daremo dropped it brusquely, his arms throbbing and nearly useless. The Ninja Master grunted as his abused bones seemed to grind against one another. The women surrounded him, their maternal instincts rising above their brutalization.

Daremo was alone for a moment, even among the women. He saw Archer in the church cell being tended by the holy man. He saw the still forms of Rhea and Hama facedown in the mud. Just two more bodies amid dozens of corpses.

"Just wait, my dear," he whispered to his love, the beautiful, unconscious Japanese woman, "your time will come."

To everything there is a season . . .

Daremo felt a grittiness in the corner of his eyes. He would be all right in a matter of minutes. He would find the camp's radio and get Bender's battalion *and* his air support in here. But when Archer recuperated, when Rhea and Hama woke up, he, the Ninja Master, would be gone.

The Season of Lava was over. He saw an image in his brain. The Season of Sand had started.